Burning Rose

Burning Rose

Shirley Kennett

Five Star • Waterville, Maine

Copyright © 2002 by Shirley Kennett

Five Star First Edition Mystery Series.

Published in 2002 in conjunction with Tekno Books and Ed Gorman.

Set in 11 pt. Plantin by Minnie B. Raven.

Printed in the United States on permanent paper.

Library of Congress Cataloging-in-Publication Data

Kennett, Shirley.
    Burning rose / Shirley Kennett.
        p. cm. — (Five Star first edition mystery series)
    ISBN 0-7862-3661-2 (hc : alk. paper)
    1. Americans—South America—Fiction.   2. Women journalists—Fiction.   3. South America—Fiction.
4. Rain forests—Fiction.   I. Title.   II. Series.
PS3561.E432 B87 2002
    813'.54—dc21   2001058591

To my true love and husband, Dennis,

and

to Ed Gorman,
who inspires me with his friendship
and his outstanding novels and stories.
Ed, you're a class act.

For every man the world is as fresh as it was
   at the first day,
And as full of untold novelties for him who has the
   eyes to see them.

> —Thomas Henry Huxley,
> English biologist,
> 1825–1895

Chapter One

"Sorry, your credit limit on this account has been exceeded. Do you want to pay with a different account?" The computerized voice managed to convey condescension.

Casey Washington frowned at her computer monitor, which displayed only the GlobeCom logo. "I've been trying to tell you I'm having a minor problem right now. Can't we work this thing out?"

"Your grace period for payment has expired. Your account has been referred to an authorized collection agency. As required by communications regulations, service to your household remains active at the basic access level. You may voice-activate 911 for emergency service, and key in all other communications. Effective immediately, all optional features are discontinued." The logo disappeared, replaced by a gray screen filled with text:

GlobeCom - Hawaii appreciates your business. Call terminated.

"Shit," said Casey. Sure, basic service was free, but nobody stayed at basic level unless it was that or starve. And that was a tough choice, especially for a journalist who depended on contact with the outside world for a living. She fished around in the capacious drawers of her battered metal desk and came up with a small keyboard that had seen better days. Sweeping aside the first level of clutter, she created a space on the desktop, enough to hold the keyboard without dumping it on the floor. She plugged it into the rear of the computer.

Grimacing, she typed in the phone number for Kenny Richards at AmerNet. She glanced at the time display in the corner of the screen. 6:05 p.m. No wonder she was hungry—she hadn't eaten since breakfast, and that had only been a couple of slices of bread smeared with chunky peanut butter. It was a little after eleven, Eastern time. Mentally she crossed her fingers that Kenny would still be there.

He probably would. Since his latest divorce he'd been spending a lot of time at work.

There was something sticky on the space bar, and sometimes the shift key stuck, making her words more emphatic than intended.

Call answered appeared on the screen. There was a pause while Kenny located his keyboard. He'd been alerted that the incoming call wasn't a voice call. The tips of Casey's ears burned with embarrassment. Now someone else knew her status, probably the first of many people. She had to go on working or she'd never get those GlobeCom options back. Letters crawled across her screen.

Yeah?

"Hi, Kenny," she typed. "It's Case. You moonlighting or on AmerNet's nickel?"

Casey hoped that Kenny would be tactful enough not to comment on her lowly phone status, or if he did, at least not notice the results of the erratic keyboard.

Jesus, kid, you back on basic? What'd you do to your keyboard? Spill syrup in it? When are you going to let me marry you and take you away from all this?

"All what?"

Virginity. Poverty. Freelancing. In that order.

"How'd you get the idea I'm still a virgin?"

Goes with your sweet face.

"A lot you know. Listen, Kenny, you said you could get something for me if I needed it. I'm sort of between assignments. Is that offer still open?"

Sure, Case. Got just the thing. Had you in mind for it all along.

There was a pause, and she pictured him rummaging around in the job jar that occupied a corner of his desk.

Yeah, right here. Perfect.

"Give me the bad news."

You like Rio? Hot nights? Nude beaches?

"What's the catch?"

It's a profile-on-location piece. Sunday supplement crap.

"God, Kenny, have I sunk so low?"

Don't knock it, sweetheart, it's the grease under the wheel of the advertising machine. The victim is Robert Gunner.

"The Robert Gunner? Of World Power?"

You got it. The corporation is starting construction on a dam someplace in Brazil. You go to Rio and then into the jungle, to the actual site. Snakes, natives, the whole bit.

"I heard about that project. You know I don't go for that. The whole thing's an ecological disaster."

Boss wants this piece real bad. Top dollar, open expenses, and maybe a follow-up when the dam's done.

"Looks like one of my alternate personas is going to Rio. Use a phony byline, something without Trixie in it this time, please. When do I pack?"

Not so fast, Case. There is one teensy little catch. You've got to land the interview yourself.

Casey sat back in her chair and sighed. There's always something.

"Kenny, how in hell am I supposed to get an interview with Gunner? He eats freelancers for breakfast, lunch and dinner. Not to mention bedtime snacks."

Should be only a minor challenge for a resourceful pro like yourself. I'll transfer an advance over to you as soon as you set up a time with him.

"Don't hold your breath."

Good luck, Case. Send photos, preferably of you at the nude beach.

"You old lecher. Thanks for the piece."

Anything for you, sweetie. You know that.

Casey tapped the termination key. She stood up and began pacing around her third floor studio apartment. It wasn't much of a place—rents on Maui were unbelievable—but it was only a block to the beach, and the view was great, if the rooftop air conditioning units of the two-story apartment house next door were ignored. Outside the salt-heavy air hung like something tangible, a cottony cloud that stung the nostrils and made a person aware of every tiny break in the skin. Inside, the space was tiny and jammed with boxes, books, and stacks of old magazines. There was little furniture, and what there was showed a serious disregard for the conventions of decorating. Other than a cramped kitchen and a double bed on the floor in the living room, the rest was given over to work. Casey had few possessions, and none that tied her down. The same could be said of her relationships.

Casey was thirty-five years old and tall enough to see eye-to-eye with most men. She had an athletic build, fair skin, and a sprinkle of freckles across her nose. Long blond hair rested in a heavy braid down the center of her back, the style unchanged since her college days. Large blue eyes with golden brown lashes dominated her slightly rounded face. She was wearing a loose T-shirt and there was a ragged hole in an intriguing portion of her cutoff jeans that she kept meaning to patch. Her girl-next-door appearance smoothed the way for her sometimes, and she wasn't above using her charm to get over, under, or around obstacles. She drew the line at the bedroom door, though.

There had been a series of men who'd made it past that

line, none of them Mr. Right. The relationships would start out fine and then turn sour, mostly over the fact that they were never alone. Her career was the third point of a love triangle.

Casey went back to the screen and did a little research, then cleared her personal ID so the recipient of her next call would not immediately know who placed it. She looked up the number for World Power, Inc., and keyed it in before she could think of all the reasons not to.

The first level of defense, as at all the megacorporations, was Public Relations. There was no discernible pause as the answerer adjusted and responded at basic level.

Good evening. Thank you for calling World Power, Inc., your source for creative solutions to energy needs. How may I help you?

The battle is joined, Casey thought. She decided on a direct approach and tried to type confidently, hoping the erratic keyboard would come across as a transmissions glitch and wouldn't make her seem like a kook.

"I want to speak to Robert Gunner."

One moment, please, I'll transfer you to his administrative assistant.

The administrative assistant, like all of the public interface points to World Power and the other megacorporations, was not a real person. It was a computer program, a glorified menu that responded to callers' choices. But it had all the stubbornness and arrogance of its human predecessor. With considerable persistence and a good deal of outright lying she reached Gunner's appointment secretary program.

Defense level two, Casey thought.

"I want to set up a meeting with your boss."

Please identify yourself and state the purpose of meeting.

"I'm Sonya Wanton and the purpose of the meeting is

none of your damn business."

Casey had claimed to be a wildly popular movie actress, a voluptuous redhead who scampered through scenes designed to maximize her obvious talents and minimize such trifles as dialogue and plot. There was no immediate response from the appointment secretary program. Casey was counting on its fuzzy logic, the programmed-in ability to handle ambiguities, to get her through this.

She knew what was running through its little microchip brain. Would the real Sonya Wanton deliberately erase her personal ID and call from an obscure location on Maui? The last public record of the actress's location indicated attendance at a party in London two days ago. Casey knew that; she'd already checked. There was ample time for the actress to surface in Hawaii. No travel records under that name, but public figures frequently traveled under a different name. Why would a movie actress want to meet with Gunner for a reason she was unwilling to state? Why would this particular movie actress, one with no publicized business acumen, want to meet with Gunner at all? How badly would Gunner react if the meeting was denied and it turned out that he would have approved it? What if the meeting turned out to be a waste of time? The program was probably considering checking with Gunner personally, but that would reflect lack of confidence in its own decision-making capacity.

Ms. Wanton, Mr. Gunner is free for lunch at the Garden of the Seven Orchids Restaurant at 12:30 p.m. Bangkok time Friday, August 30. He would be pleased if you would join him there. Please indicate if this is acceptable.

"I'll be there."

Now Casey just had to get Kenny to free up money for reservations to Bangkok.

Piece of cake.

Chapter Two

Albert Gantry was a hat and raincoat man, so he didn't have the excuse of an umbrella blocking his view. He did have his head tilted down, walking from the conference site to Saul's Deli, and that accounted for the collision with the woman.

She came from a storefront with a green awning and leaded glass door. He saw her from the corner of his eye, but momentum ruled the moment.

Gantry rebounded slightly and dropped his briefcase into a puddle. She fell over backward, landing hard on the curb. Her purse flew in a trajectory reminiscent of charts in physics textbooks with bullets traveling from Point A to Point B. As the purse hit the ground and splattered its contents, her shoe fell off into the rain-filled gutter.

"Oh, sorry, my fault." He bent over to offer her a hand up, and the rain accumulated in the brim of his hat poured down the front of her dress. She scrambled to her feet, breathless. The umbrella was a tragic sight, ribs askew. She struggled with it and succeeded only in poking a hole in her dress.

"Please, wait under the awning out of the rain," he said, "and I'll retrieve your things."

"I'm so sorry. I just didn't see you." Her voice was a natural melody, like a gentle rain striking a pond.

"My fault, I assure you," Gantry said. He reached for the contents of her purse, a collection of small shiny objects that perversely rolled away from him. As an afterthought he retrieved her shoe from the gutter. He stepped under the awning and got his first good look at the woman. She was Asian and lovely.

It wasn't so much a look as a sensory impression. The damp, fresh, female smell of her, the soft music of her voice, the cool touch of her fingers as she accepted the soggy items. Thin dress, wet from the rain, clinging to her body—she might as well have been naked. Firm calves, no stockings. One delicate, bare foot with perfect red painted toenails. Straight dark hair, just long enough to graze her shoulders, slick against her neck. Blood-red lips and eyes black enough for a man to get lost in and never find his way out.

She smiled as she slung the purse strap over her shoulder and tilted the shoe, dumping out some water. As she turned and bent to slip her shoe on, her buttocks, clearly defined under the wet dress, pressed momentarily against his hip. He reluctantly tore his eyes away and moved to pick up his briefcase.

The thought came to him that she was seriously underdressed for the weather.

"Your dress is ruined," Gantry said with a small catch in his throat. "You must allow me to pay for it."

"How gallant! But perhaps it would be more fun if you offered me your clothes in exchange," she said. There was a faint trace of British accent in her voice, probably acquired during her schooling. "Come inside and we'll dry each other off."

She turned back to the shop door, fished around in her wet purse and pulled out a set of keys. She stepped inside the darkened shop. An old-fashioned bell tinkled above the door, a charming anachronism.

Gantry, reacting to the dual mental images of exchanging clothes and drying her off, felt his cheeks burning. He hesitated, hand on the doorknob. She turned around impatiently, then her face softened when she saw the flush in his cheeks.

"Please come in. I was only kidding about the clothes. I'm not planning to strip you just yet." She flipped on the lights and the interior of the store glowed warmly. Gantry picked up her umbrella, stepped in and closed the door behind him, shutting out the noise of the storm and the traffic. It was a flower shop, and every inch of counter space was filled with fresh blooms in beautiful arrangements. The heavy, humid air was saturated with dozens of different scents.

She disappeared behind a curtain at the back of the shop. Her voice drifted out.

"I'll be back in a minute. Have a look around." A folded-up towel sailed out from behind the curtain and landed on the crowded countertop without upsetting a single vase.

"Good shot," he said. He was rewarded with a muffled giggle, the kind of sound she might make when pulling a dress over her head. Gantry derailed that train of thought. He toweled himself quickly, absorbing some drips from his hat and raincoat and mopping his briefcase dry. Time passed, and he wondered if he should quietly leave. Instead, he examined the shop, looking at the floral arrangements. To his unpracticed eye, they seemed exceptionally good. He noticed a camera in a corner near the ceiling, red light blinking, to deter shoplifters. The heat rose in his cheeks again at the thought that she, naked behind the curtain, might be watching him on the camera. It wasn't lost on him that the windows and the glass door were tightly covered with shades.

He was on his second circuit of the shop when the curtains parted. She was encased in a white terry cloth bathrobe, overlapped and cinched in no-nonsense fashion in front. Her hair was damp and glistening, and there was a spot of redness in each cheek, probably the aftermath of a hot shower. She carried a tray with a tea set.

"I know it's a bit early for tea, but I thought something hot would do us both good."

"Thank you, but I must be going. Are you sure you won't let me pay for your clothing?"

"Don't be silly. It's all washable. It'll be as good as new."

"How about this?" he said. He held up the smashed umbrella. "I think it's a goner."

"Stay and have some tea, and we'll call it even."

Gantry gave in. "All right."

He slipped out of his raincoat and pulled a stool up to the counter opposite her. Spoons clinked, sugar swirled. A simple cup of tea had never seemed so sensual. Over tiny seed cakes, their eyes met and held for a long silent moment, hers unwavering, his averted at last.

"A very pleasant shop," he said to fill the empty space in the conversation. "Do you work here?"

"It's all mine, such as it is," she answered. "I've always loved to work with flowers. Some say I have a real touch with them, especially roses. There's a small apartment in back, just a couple of rooms, so I live here too. At least until I can get myself a bigger place."

"You're ambitious, then."

"Not really. All I want is a chain of shops and a ten-room apartment overlooking Central Park," she said. "How about you? What do you do?"

"Government service," Gantry answered. "Environmental Protection Agency in Washington. There's an international conference going on. I lobbied for Amsterdam, but New York won the toss this year." It appeared she hadn't recognized him. His face had been plastered over the newspapers lately, since he was the head of the EPA.

"You don't look nearly stodgy enough to be in government service. Or like one of those eco-fanatics, either."

"Thank you, I think." Gantry was forty-six years old, trim and fit from daily workouts.

"Married?" She dropped the question between them. He hesitated just long enough to earn himself a quizzical look.

"Happily," he said. "Almost twenty years. Two daughters." He couldn't seem to form a clear picture of his wife Mary's face in his mind. When he tried, he saw only black eyes, blood-red lips. He watched a drop of water fall from her straight dark hair and vanish into the terry cloth.

"Too bad. This place would make a great mom-and-pop business."

Once again, their eyes found each other. After a moment he drained the last drops of tea, and reached for his raincoat and hat. She walked around the end of the counter, passing a magnificent arrangement of red roses. Picking up a gleaming pair of scissors, she snipped the rose from the center, the one that was elevated above the others, the single perfect flower to be claimed for a man's lapel.

Suddenly she was close, very close, the top of her head just below his chin. Her scent drifted up to his nostrils, mingling with the overall fragrance in the shop, but distinctive, delicious . . . arousing. His hands rested lightly on her waist for a moment. Her bathrobe shifted, and he caught a glimpse of a tattoo between her breasts, a delicate rose, a lifelike work of art done by a master. Then the gown shifted again, and he wondered if he'd really seen it. She took a step back and surveyed her handiwork, the red rose lodged in his lapel. She patted his chest in approval, then reached up and tapped her finger playfully on his lips.

"You're the type for a flaming red rose, you know. Not everyone can wear them," she said. "It says something about the inner person, don't you think?"

Gantry slipped his raincoat on, crisscrossing the buttons and having to start over.

"Thanks for the tea," he managed to say.

"It was nice bumping into you. If there's anything else I can do for you . . . flowers and such, you know where to find me."

At the door, he remembered he hadn't even introduced himself. "I'm Albert Gantry, by the way."

"Rose Shikuru. Pleased to meet you."

He nodded. He could feel the rose on his lapel as a tiny spot of warmth on his chest, like a candle flame under the raincoat. The bell over the door tinkled, and he was on his way back to the conference, lunch forgotten.

And from there, home to Washington, D.C., and to Mary.

Days passed, stretched into weeks, and he did not see Rose again. But the candle flame she had placed under his coat grew as though someone were carefully blowing on it, encouraging it.

Gantry dove into his work, trying to wipe her image from his mind. Hot spots of environmental concern flared regularly, mainly dealing with megacorps. World Power controlled energy production and distribution. Tamura Products manufactured consumer goods, from clothing to appliances. GlobeCom handled worldwide voice and data communication. Superior Services dealt with the myriad processes of daily life, from the humblest chain of laundry mats on up. Frontier Enterprises was for those who lived on the edge: undersea and space exploration—and exploitation.

Gantry was engaged in a complex dance with Superior Services. Their latest proposal placed a luxury resort for the ultra-rich on one of the last unspoiled wetlands in southern Florida. Or more precisely, over one of the last unspoiled wetlands, since it was to be housed in a hovering dome suspended on columns of air with the potential energy of bottled tornadoes. And the effect of continuous tornadoes, below the surface of the water. To Harley Bentson, CEO of Superior Services, that was not a problem, because the Florida wetlands were just soggy hunks of land with a lot of mosquitoes.

Gantry had allowed himself to be won over for the project. He knew that the dome technology just wasn't there yet. Even if Superior managed to pull the technological rabbit out of the hat, Gantry rationalized, the wetlands would be just one more lost battle in a war fought on many fronts. In the meantime, the good will he was putting in the bank might avert some even worse situation.

The extra money didn't hurt either.

If Gantry were truly honest with himself, he would not have been surprised to find himself standing in front of Rose's flower shop on a sultry day in late summer. As it was, he thought that it was quite a coincidence that he needed flowers for his wedding anniversary, and here he was standing in front of a flower shop with a green awning that arched over the window as if to protect the interior from prying eyes.

Inside the shop it was dim and cool. Again, the shades were drawn, he supposed against the heat of the afternoon. He looked around and remembered it all as though the intervening days had not existed. The cheerful ring of the bell brought her from the back of the shop, through the curtains. She wore an ankle-length sundress, flowered in pastel shades, which bared her arms and buttoned all the way down from neckline to hemline. A tantalizing number of buttons were already undone, top and bottom. There was recognition and welcome in her face and voice. Because of that, a thought began to form in his mind that it had been the same for her—that she had been waiting for him to walk through that door again, that time had stopped for her too.

"I need some flowers." He cleared his throat. "For our wedding anniversary."

"You've certainly come to the right place, Mr. Gantry, although you didn't have to come here in person. I do a lot of business by phone. I'm delighted to see you again, though. When is the happy event?"

"Tomorrow. I know it's short notice, but I'm sure you could whip up something. Something . . . big." He paused, mortified that she might interpret a double meaning in what he had just blurted out. But her expression was placid, so he continued. "And please call me Albert."

She moved toward a refrigerator case that held several vases, each with a "hold" tag, and buckets of loose flowers. He was surprised to see that she was barefoot, toenails painted vivid red, as they had been when he last glimpsed them. He was a man with a mind for detail.

"Tell me about her," she said.

"Pardon?"

"Tell me a little about your wife, so that I can choose the flowers."

"Oh," Gantry said. He was mesmerized by the view as she walked away from him. The dress was backless, to a point just far enough above the swell of her buttocks to conceal the mysterious separation between them. He swallowed hard.

"She's older than you, taller, with light hair. Gray eyes, I think."

She turned and gave him a mock exasperated look. "I mean tell me about the way she is, not the way she looks. Romantic, nostalgic, calculating, impetuous, that sort of thing."

He chose his words carefully. "She used to be quite a romantic. We both were."

She raised her delicate eyebrows. "A romantic spirit never dies. It simply waits for the right situation to express itself."

She opened the case and bent over to reach a large bucket of white roses near the back, speaking to him over her shoulder. "How about white roses, for purity of mind and body?"

With a few quick steps he was behind her. Although she must have felt his closeness, she remained bent at the waist. He put both hands on her shoulders and drew them slowly down her bare back, thumbs tracing her spine. She tensed, but didn't move away. His hands came to rest on the satisfying flare of her hips. He bent over her, molding his body to hers. He could feel the tightness in her abdomen, the smooth firmness, the muscles clenching with anticipation. His hands traveled slowly up the front of her and cupped her breasts.

Through the fog of his lust, he remembered where he was. In a public shop. With an unlocked door. He pulled himself away and moved toward the door to lock it.

"No," she said. Velvet voice. "Leave it open."

As he turned, erection pointing the way, he happened to notice the camera high up in the corner, red light blinking.

But then she was in front of him, unzipping his trousers, unbuttoning her dress. His attention was riveted on her hands. When her fingers reached a button below waist level, she slid the dress down over her hips. She stood naked in the dimness, her dark triangle vulnerable to him, the skin painting of a red rose again revealed in the private place between her breasts. Then she began to move, swaying her hips enticingly. She danced so close to him he could feel her body heat, that fire she had between her legs and everywhere else inside her. But when he reached for her, she moved away. He became aware that she was humming an unfamiliar, almost childish, tune. His breathing grew shallow and fast as he watched her. When she reached the end of her tune, she came to a stop in front of him. She put her arms up, her hands behind his neck. In one graceful motion of her dancer's body, she lifted herself, entwined her legs around his hips, took him inside, and continued her rhythmic motion.

Mary had never done that.

When he left the shop, he carried the memory of an incredible erotic experience, and a large box of white roses with baby's breath. He returned whenever he could manage, drawn like a hummingbird to the sweetness of nectar. No matter what exotic and varied foreplay she had in mind, there was always the humming and the dance. He never asked her about it. It was part of the whole, and it was the whole of her he craved. The tune stayed in his mind, and he could get an erection at any time just by humming it to himself.

The door was always unlocked. By chance no customers ever entered the shop in those heated, intense moments.

But they could have.

It added a delicious twist that he had never sampled

prior to Rose. In all the years of his marriage, he had been faithful to his wife, in deed if not in thought, until now. As for the moral issue, the fidelity part, it slipped from his grasp with surprising ease. He was a man caught in the throes of a mid-life affair, passion eclipsing the comfortable companionship of his marriage.

He knew without a doubt that love played no part in it for her. She was a creature of lust and abandon, the kind that a man would feel grateful to encounter once in his life. That was also delicious in its way, since it meant that there was actually no threat to his marriage, no worry about all the complications there would be in his career if he should run off with a woman with red toenails a couple of decades his junior.

But if he couldn't have her love, then her body was enough. There was no thought in his mind of ending it, of changing their relationship in any way. She was New York; Mary was Washington.

He resumed his work with his old fervor, so much so that his colleagues noticed his renewed enthusiasm and assumed that the payoff payments were arriving regularly from Superior Services, Inc. As a matter of fact, they were.

On a weekend trip to New York, he impulsively stopped at the flower shop. It was closed, of course, but he knocked his special two knocks, pause, three more. She opened the door, sleepy-eyed and wearing one of his shirts as a nightshirt. Without a word she drew him inside, pulling him from the cold night into the warmth of her embrace. When he was ready to leave, she darted behind the curtain.

"Don't go yet. I have something for you."

He waited, and she came back with a black velvet box. "Open it," she said. In the box was an exquisite red silk rose with one green leaf.

"I made it myself," she said, "so you can look like a real gentleman even when you can't come to my shop." He was touched. It was the only thing she had given him, other than her body. He stood patiently, in a state of dreamy satiation, while she tucked the silk stem into his lapel.

"Good-bye, Albert," she said. "Sweet dreams . . ."

A warm wave of satisfaction moved through Rose in spite of the shop's middle-of-the-night chill. Two minutes, one, boom! She headed for her bedroom, back behind the curtains. The sirens were fast in sounding, and seemed to be converging from a wide area. Gunfire on the streets of New York might not draw a rapid response any more, but explosions still were novel enough.

Chapter Three

Starlight streamed down into the darkened conference room in the Swiss Alps and fell, without a hint of judgment, upon six upturned faces. The conference room was large, its borders undefined in the darkness. A domed skylight, twenty feet or more across, was echoed below by a round table that precisely matched the dome's diameter.

Five figures sat in the shadows at the table's edge. A sixth stood apart. A spotlight came on, forming a harsh cone of light illuminating one of the figures at the table. The tabletop itself was revealed as a massive slab of polished granite that seemed to absorb any light insolent enough to stray onto its surface. The figure, a man in an artfully executed clown costume, seemed out of place in the somber and dramatic surroundings. He wore bright yellow loose-fitting trousers, held up chest-high with ludicrous suspenders, over a purple shirt with sleeves that ballooned out from his shoulders. A rainbow wig topped his head, and he sported a classic red bulb nose. Drawn on his cheek in black greasepaint was an exaggerated tear. At the center of the tear, a large diamond flashed in the spotlight. The man reached up and pinched his red nose. It honked, a crass noise under the stars.

"I am Tearful Clown, and this is my story . . ."

He spoke in a rich, commanding voice, a voice others would hurry to obey. Tearful Clown told a lengthy story of outrages and the actions he had taken to stop them. It was the story of his graduation years ago from activism to ex-

27

tremism, an awakening of sorts. The four others seated at the table had heard this story before, most of them multiple times. It was new only to the one person standing apart. There had been many actions since that awakening, but Tearful Clown always related the first. He had paid his dues that time. He had qualified for membership in The Six.

When he reached the conclusion there was a collective sigh, a release of breath, of tension. It was as though the telling of the first story loosened things, made it easier to shift the line between right and wrong to a more accommodating point.

One by one, as the spotlights came on around the table, the others told of their initiations. Chess Master, gowned in a flowing purple robe with golden edges, a king's golden crown gleaming in the spotlight, face hidden behind a stylized actor's mask. Cold-Blooded Serpent, iridescent scales caressing her sinuous body and spilling onto her face. Wrongful Death, in a nightmarish costume any Trick-or-Treater would envy, with a skull face and an arrestingly realistic open chest cavity. Playful Cat, dark skin melting into a body suit that followed every line of his muscular frame, with perfect orange stripes, and a cat mask complete with whiskers and a pink nose pad.

Finally, a cone of light descended upon an empty chair. There was a moment of silence as the five mourned the former occupant. Tearful Clown spoke the first words of the initiation ritual, the means by which The Six filled empty chairs.

"Step forward and speak. This night you join us or die."

The standing figure moved forward into the light, but did not sit down. She wore a floor-length red gown that laced from the high neckline to just below her navel. The laces were thin golden threads that did not seem adequate to contain her breasts and hips. The red fabric was covered with tiny crystals that caught the light and flamed yellow with every movement, a bright yellow, not like the subtle yellow cast of her skin. A red mask, encrusted with the same crystals, covered the top half of her face. Black eyes glittered from slits in the mask. Below the mask her lips were blood red and the corners of her mouth were turned up in an unreadable smile. Nestled in the warm, fragrant spot between her breasts was a skin painting of a perfect red rose in early bloom. She stretched her arms forward as if to embrace those seated at the table, a triumphant gesture that did not acknowledge Tearful Clown's threat. As she moved, her gown flashed, and it seemed to the onlookers that she was consumed in wind-blown flames. Her voice was as soft as a rose petal.

"I am Burning Rose, and this is my story."

When Rose ended her tale she stood proudly in her cone of light. She waited for the full effect of her graphically told story of lust and betrayal, of a man in government service who took bribes, and a flower shop with a green awning, to be felt.

"Have I earned my place at this table?"

One by one, the other five nodded.

"You have," said Tearful Clown. "Be seated, Burning Rose. There is an immediate assignment for you. Are you prepared to take action in the name of The Six?"

Below the crystal mask, the tip of her tongue lazily swept across her red lips, as though savoring the last remnants of some unnatural meal. The Milky Way splayed across the night sky above the domed skylight, cold and indifferent.

"Isn't that what I'm here for?"

Chapter Four

The trip from Maui to Bangkok was uneventful. Casey traveled Thrifty Tourist class, the lowliest of the low, even though Kenny had transferred a sum into her account that made her eyes light up. She saved money on the flight in order to blow some of it on a spectacular new dress, custom fitted in her hotel room. It hurt to see that money flowing from her fingertips, but her usual wardrobe didn't seem appropriate for something called the Garden of the Seven Orchids. She had time for a long hot bath and a nap before the lunch date.

As a pleasant surprise, her room was equipped with a positively decadent personal spa. She tossed her clothes on the bed, twirled the knob to "The Works," and stepped into the cubicle. An hour later, she emerged thoroughly relaxed, skin fairly gleaming, ready for anything, even lunch with one of the most influential men in the world.

A lunch date obtained by cheating the system.

Some explanation would be expected, that is if he didn't just get up and leave. She didn't have anything rehearsed. Casey always did think fast on her feet.

But she wasn't on her feet when her alarm went off, an old-fashioned windup with a shrill sound that went beyond annoying into the realm of masochistic. It took several minutes for her to piece together where she was and why. Splashing some cold water on her face accelerated the process. She cupped her hand to collect some of the water, and used it to swallow a jetlag pill she'd forgotten to take upon arrival. She pulled on some socks and exercise shoes, leaving the rest of her body bare, the same way that she slept.

Then she slipped a tape into her audio recorder and adjusted the volume. The device, which fit into the palm of her hand, was one of the most important pieces of equipment a freelancer used. There was a spare tucked into her luggage. This time, the machine wasn't set to silently record. Instead, it was on playback, and the tape she'd inserted was an exercise routine. Rhythmic music filled the air, and she became absorbed in her exercise, reveling in the physical abandon of it.

When the room was silent again, she took a quick cold shower, braided her hair and piled it on top of her head, drew on her new dress and sandals, and fastened a matching travel bag around her trim waist. The tiny bag held some Thai currency, a comb, and a lipstick. She placed a blank tape into her recorder, slipped the little unit into the bag, and patted the bag's closure.

Casey decided to soak up local color—never know when these things would come in handy, and her budget didn't permit flitting off to Thailand on a whim. She opted for a tuk-tuk instead of an air-conditioned tourist taxi, and regretted it immediately. Tuk-tuks were small open vehicles named after the puttering noise made by their engines. The streets were noisy, hectic, and very smelly. Noxious air pollution was churned out by belching buses and her own tuk-tuk, which coughed and died at each corner, necessitating much cursing and banging of fists by the driver as he urged the recalcitrant engine back to life. The city hadn't changed at all since the last time she was here, ten years ago at least. In fact, she now remembered, she had been here for a party as a teenager. Her boyfriend had been an industrialist's son and he'd had access to a private jet. None of her recent men friends had jets. She'd have to work on that.

The humidity, heat, and drizzle of rain sapped her resolve and frizzed her hair so that her blonde braids took on a fuzzy appearance. Loose strands curled wetly on her forehead and neck. By the time she reached the restaurant she was uncharacteristically tense. She snapped at the driver because he pulled up too far from the curb, causing her to disembark into a dirty puddle. Casey paid the driver the fare they had negotiated before she even entered the tuk-tuk, thrusting the hundred-baht note into his face through the open window. He shrugged and pulled away without a backward glance.

Farang. Foreigner. She knew he was thinking it, and at the moment didn't care if he thought she was a witch or a baby-stealer.

Once inside, Casey made a beeline for the ladies' room, where she stood for a moment just letting the cool air refresh her. Then she quickly dabbed her lips with her Red Licorice lipstick, the only makeup she used. As she checked her face in the mirror, she suddenly began to doubt the whole thing. Was she, a person who always voted for the Eco Party candidate, a fifteen-year member of the Consortium for the Planet, really going to have lunch with the enemy? Even worse, was she going to write a piece promoting, or at least not fervently objecting to, the Brazilian power project? Maybe she could turn it into a pure profile of Bob Gunner, the man, leaving out the dam altogether.

Is this the first chink in the wall, that erosion of ideals to pay the GlobeCom bill?

Or was she just getting too old—forty was looming large in her mind, even though she had a few birthdays left before that—for that golden glow of righteousness?

"Let's just fly by the seat of our pants, as usual," she said to her reflection in the mirror.

The restaurant was a visual delight. There were tropical plants everywhere, and the tables were placed among them on many levels, so that the impression was of dining in a treehouse. Shafts of sunlight streamed in from several skylights but did not reach far into the depths, a faithful rendition of sunlight struggling to reach the forest floor through the canopy overhead. Each table was edged in a band of tiny lights that sparkled in the dim, cool places deep in the shadows of foliage. Soft forest noises, birds and insects, played in the background. The memory of the trip through the streets outside faded from Casey's mind as she took in the view. She gave her name as Sonya Wanton, and was ushered to Gunner's table.

He had arrived before her and was using a phone. As he saw her approaching he ended his conversation, and the phone folded away into a tabletop niche to await the next customer's request.

He stood as she came near, his eyes traveling down and back up her body with interest, but no recognition. He nodded slightly, pulled out her chair and seated her. Casey's gaze fastened on the small candle in the center of the table. When he was seated, she raised her eyes to look him over. Broad shoulders, perfectly fitted shirt and jacket. Brown hair with an overall silver cast. A presence of authority that radiated from him almost visibly, like heat waves from the top of a working toaster. Not the sort of person she could comfortably call Bob. Robert or Mr. Gunner, but never Bob.

Faced with his formidable presence, she began to lose confidence. All she could think of for a moment was that her hair was frizzy and the neckline of her dress was low, too low.

A man detached himself from a nearby table and sauntered toward them. His appearance was menacing, even
though he was smiling. When he arrived at their table, he
kept his eyes on Casey while speaking to Gunner.

"Anything I can do for you, sir?" he said.

Casey realized that he was Gunner's bodyguard, or one
of them at least. There was probably at least one more
among the restaurant's customers, as backup. She sighed.

At least I got this far. Good-bye, expense account.

"No thanks, Reggie. I think I can handle this on my
own. Enjoy your lunch."

"Yes, sir." Reggie looked at Casey appraisingly and
grinned.

She looked away, embarrassed, realizing what Reggie
was thinking in connection with Gunner's statement about
handling her on his own.

"You aren't Sonya, but you'll do until she comes along,"
Gunner said. Casey could feel a flush rising in her cheeks.

"Mr. Gunner, I'm sorry about this deception. It's just
that I . . . I needed to meet you. I'm a freelance writer, and
I accepted an assignment to do a profile piece on you. I
didn't think you'd see me if I said who I really was."

"A writer, then?" He sounded a little disappointed. She
nodded. "I must have a chat with that appointment secretary of mine," he said. "Well, as long as I'm here and you're
here, we might as well have lunch. How about it?"

"I think that would be just fine. My name's Casey, by
the way, Casey Washington." He smiled, and Casey smiled
back in spite of herself.

Watch it, girl. Remember, this guy is the enemy.

With a delicious meal of vegetable curry resting in her
contented stomach, Casey ran her finger around the edge of
her coffee cup. There had been considerable conversation

during lunch, but only neutral topics like the weather and places to visit in Bangkok. World Power's headquarters were in Thailand, and Gunner had a private wing of the ultramodern complex as his own living quarters. He knew the city well, all the fascinating stuff you don't run up against on a tourist hop. Casey was sure he had a lot of interesting stories to tell. But right now she was interested in just one, the one she needed for her assignment. Gunner was a charismatic man, and she had to continually remind herself that the things he and his company stood for were not her cup of tea. This was strictly for money. A few pages under a fake byline, and nothing to connect her with the evil deed.

It had been years since Casey had landed an assignment with open expenses. Such things didn't come along often in the activist press. It felt good to know that the money for travel and meals wasn't coming out of her shallow pockets. Throughout lunch, they had shared pleasantries and called each other Robert and Casey like old friends who just happened to meet in this fabulous restaurant. Things were going surprisingly well. She hadn't been kicked out yet. Feeling mellow, she opened the travel bag at her waist, took out the recorder, and placed it on the table between them.

"Back to business, right? I've never known a writer whose social skills prevailed for more than an hour, so I guess the timing's just about perfect," he said.

She nodded and pressed the record button.

"Now, Mr. Gunner, perhaps you'll tell me a little about your personal involvement in the São Gabriel hydroelectric project."

She swallowed hard. The neutral opening question she had been planning to ask, had been mentally putting together for the last several minutes, concerned which cities the power was destined to supply and what a change that would make in the local economies. Something about the cascading effect of cheaper power, the eventual improvement in the local standard of living. The party line. Suddenly her mouth leapt ahead of her brain and out popped a question that wasn't going to advance the cause of paying off the GlobeCom bill.

"For starters," she said, "how do you feel about the displacement of the Guehero natives and the flooding of thousands of acres of irreplaceable rainforest?"

His gray eyes grew hard. "Exactly what sort of article are you writing, Miss Washington? And for what publication?"

So it was Miss Washington now, not Casey.

Casey sighed and leaned back in her chair. "I'm on assignment for AmerNet, and I'm supposed to be doing a piece on the white knight charging to the rescue of electricity-starved South America. Something like that."

"In that case, I don't think you'll sell the article if you slant it with the viewpoint you're taking. I wasn't aware that AmerNet had turned such a deep shade of Green overnight. Did you by any chance get this assignment through the same kind of deception you used to arrange our meeting?"

"No. I was sincere, or at least I thought I was."

"Then why did you take this assignment if you couldn't carry it out in good faith?"

Casey sifted through the options for answering that question and settled on honesty. "Simple. I needed the money, and I thought I could get out of this with minimal compromise."

"So now we're into compromise." Gunner leaned forward. "Listen, Miss Washington, I know more about compromise than you'll learn in a lifetime. It so happens I believe in what I'm doing, which is more than I can say for you." He paused and took a deep breath, visibly getting his anger under control before continuing.

"I liked you," he said. "I admired the way you got past Public Relations in the first place. I respected you for having the nerve to follow through by showing up here. If you had wanted fluff," he gestured toward the recorder, "I would cheerfully have given you fluff for your article. If you wanted a real debate on ecology issues, I would have given you that, but your mind is already snapped shut. You sold out your principles for a few bucks."

He rose from the table. As he did so, his bodyguard glided smoothly to his side. The two men exchanged a brief look, and Gunner walked away. Reggie reached down and picked up the recorder. His hand closed over it and squeezed. When he opened his fist, crushed pieces fell out onto the table.

"Guess the interview's over, Miss." He moved away and caught up with Gunner, who was standing near the door with his back turned. Another customer, a woman, abruptly rose and joined them. So there was another personal guard in the room. Smugness over being right on one small point was all that was left to Casey at that moment.

She sat at the table a while longer. When she finally stood up and left, tears spilled from her eyes. Out on the street, hailing a tuk-tuk to get herself back to the hotel, she wiped furiously at her eyes. She ignored the hair-raising ride, lost in a re-enactment of the last few minutes of her lunch with Robert Gunner. She wished she had said something clever and cutting at the end. She was keenly aware that he had gotten the last word, and in grand style at that.

That wasn't the only problem. How was she going to do the piece for AmerNet? She had already drawn upon the advance Kenny had given her for travel and expenses, and now she had nothing to offer, not even Gunner's voice on her recorder. That dinosaur of a bodyguard had crushed the hell out of it. Oh, sure, she could dig up some tired facts from previously published articles about the man. Or paraphrase a press release from World Power itself. Kenny might even accept it, but both of them would know that it wasn't the work she was capable of doing. The next time she called Kenny, his phone answering service would probably inform her that he was "in a meeting." And the next time, and the next time, until she got the hint.

How could she salvage this? She pulled her thoughts away from all the things she should have said. When she stepped out of the little vehicle, once again splashing into a puddle at the curb, she knew exactly what she was going to do.

She was going to do what she did best, activist writing. If AmerNet didn't want it, she would sell the article somewhere else and pay Kenny back. A knockout article exposing the seamy side of World Power and most particularly of Robert Gunner. Good enough to arouse the complacent masses. Good enough to put to rest those disturbing little thoughts that Gunner might be right about compromises and where they lead.

She was afraid that if she looked closely at herself, she would find that Gunner was right about her straying too far from her ideals. And had she done so in some noble cause where she could delude herself into thinking that the end justified the means? No. It was all in the pursuit of creature comforts, of expense accounts and tailored dresses and GlobeCom options. It was easier to feel the fire of righteous indignation directed at Gunner than to admit she had somehow, with the passing of years, gotten shallow.

She got to work in her hotel room. She phoned everyone she could think of, journalists and otherwise, who might conceivably owe her a favor. She was looking for information about Gunner—no, no, she told herself, about the hydroelectric project. Something to feed the flames of her anger, something delicious and destructive. Among the two dozen or so people she contacted were some powerful and resourceful characters. The word was out. Something would turn up, and she hoped it would be soon. She couldn't sustain any scheme with Kenny for long.

Had she actually enjoyed laughing with Gunner, enjoyed his warm smile and the moment their fingertips touched when they both reached for the basket of bread at the same time?

Remember, this guy is the enemy.

Chapter Five

Gunner didn't stay angry long. In fact, by the time the V.I.P. elevator got up to the roof of the Garden of the Seven Orchids, he was feeling a little guilty for coming down so hard on Casey. But he hated to see her on the edge of selling out. If his outburst headed her off in a different direction, it was worth a little poor public relations. He grinned. He didn't get to be the man he was by winning popularity contests.

The helicopter was warmed up and ready to go when he stepped onto the rooftop pad. Evidently the pilot had been notified when he left the restaurant. Gunner's time was too valuable for mundane things like waiting for transportation.

Reggie Camden, his chief bodyguard, moved ahead of him and entered the small cabin of the modified copter. Usually, the passenger compartment was open to the pilot area, but in this one there was a divider behind the pilot's seat. The interior was finished as an office, complete with desk, computer, and phone. There was a low couch along the back wall of the cabin so that Gunner could nap while in the air, in the unlikely event that he didn't feel like working.

Once inside, the bodyguard pressed a button on a device on his belt. The single beep and then smooth hum of the gadget he wore, called a Tattletale, meant there were no explosive devices or untagged weapons aboard. Reggie's gun was "tagged," meaning it was legally registered and emitted an identifying radio frequency. The Tattletale heard it and beeped complacently, since it recognized the frequency as belonging to Reggie. If there had been unregistered weapons or explosives, or registered weapons that did not belong to Reggie, a wavering tone would have sounded.

Gunner knew if things were left up to Reggie, the man would have carried something a lot more lethal than a trangun, which fired knockout capsules. Gunner specifically required the use of tranguns, though. That way in case there was an accident or misunderstanding by his security staff in dealing with the public, at least the effects were reversible. The capsules splattered on impact and dropped an assailant with a super-fast-acting tranquilizer that was absorbed through the skin, inhaled, or taken in through the tear ducts. The liquid tranquilizer was piggybacked with a distinctive, micro-dose radioactive signature that made subsequent identification and prosecution of the marked assailant a breeze.

True, there were some problems with knockout capsules. An assailant with a dangerously high, nearly lethal, dose of stimulants circulating in his body might not drop instantaneously. But such a person would be acting erratically, and would be spotted and disabled physically. And there were body suits and filtration devices available on the undermarket that thwarted knockout capsules. Sometimes.

Reggie told the pilot their destination, which was Gunner's private suite at HQ, and remained in the pilot's compartment. Gunner settled into his comfortable chair. Tanya, the female guard who'd had her lunch interrupted in the restaurant, was staying behind. Gunner had overheard Reggie tell her to begin looking into this Casey Washington's background, to find out if she was really a penniless journalist, or if there was something another layer down that might be threatening.

As the copter lifted into the air, Gunner flicked on the scrambler. A red light on his desk indicated that his communications were secure, scrambled into white noise anywhere beyond a diameter of a couple of meters. He decided to use the few minutes of airtime to check his mail. Almost all incoming messages were routed through the administrative assistant or appointment secretary programs as necessary. Only a few came directly to his private code.

"Sally, check the mail," he said. Gunner had given all of his computerized assistants names of women, in spite of some not-so-good-natured kidding by his senior female executives-in-the-flesh. His appointment secretary was Fran, the administrative assistant was Colleen. The personal secretary program answered to the name of Sally when it was in a good mood. A beautiful young blonde appeared on the monitor and replied in a breathy voice, managing to make dry business mail sound seductive.

Chapter Six

"Good evening, Doctor Riley." The doorman nodded slightly as the elderly man with the bulging, odd-shaped package tucked under one arm negotiated the door.

"I've told you time and again, young man, to call me Warren. No sense being fancy about titles, especially one that every Tom, Dick, and Mabel can get for a smile and a C-note."

"Yes, sir, Doc, er, Warren."

"By the way, I'm expecting a rather large package tomorrow or the day after—some parts for my latest doodad."

Dr. Riley's inventions, which he modestly called his doodads, had made him far wealthier than his simple needs demanded. He still lived in the eighth floor apartment overlooking Central Park where he and his wife had spent their honeymoon. When the Sands of Time device had gone into production and the sales were phenomenal, he had briefly toyed with the idea of moving to the penthouse, most recently occupied by a disagreeable dowager with four poodles. He decided against it because he would have had to replace the carpets.

"I see," said the doorman. "And will we be needing the crane again?"

The last large package had exceeded the weight limit of the old cage-style elevator in the building, which had valiantly struggled to the sixth floor before the cables slipped. The elevator operator had the ride of his life before the manual brakes took hold at the second floor. Dr. Riley had been more irritated than apologetic, and threatened to sue the owner if the contents of his package should turn out to have so much as a scratch. Eventually a crane was summoned, a window hastily enlarged, and the crate settled in Dr. Riley's eighth floor apartment, despite the protests of a nervous seventh floor resident.

"Hardly. I would say this package will only be about so big." Dr. Riley held his hand out waist high, then started to walk toward the elevator. The doorman hurried to the reception desk, which had not been staffed for years. From the top drawer, he removed a bedraggled bouquet of flowers and offered them to the doctor.

"For Mrs. Riley . . . Dorothy, that is," said the doorman.

"Why, how nice of you to remember her birthday. I'll take these right up." He inspected the droopy blooms, wondering how long the doorman had kept them in the desk, and which other resident in the building had never received the floral delivery. "Dorothy always could do wonders with a few blossoms and a simple vase."

When Dr. Riley entered his apartment, lights came on throughout the spacious rooms. "Too bright," he said, and the lights dimmed to lend a soft ambiance. He put the package down on the kitchen counter, filled two water glasses, took a long gulp from one, and then plopped the flowers into the other. He imagined he could hear them slurping up the water, as he had. In the living room, he sat in a worn leather chair, the only place to sit in the entire room. The rest of the space was taken up with an odd assortment of tables. The tops of the tables were covered with chessboards, roughly fifty of them, all of them with games in progress.

"Play all messages," he said, "coded Game, priority one only." The computer, squeezed onto a table in a corner, coughed into obedience and rattled off a dozen messages left by other players, indicating their next move in the ongoing games. When the machine finished, Dr. Riley sipped once from his glass of water before responding. Then he dictated his own moves in response. The computer would dial the correct phone numbers later, when rates were lower. No sense spending extra. His GlobeCom bill was bad enough already, with games going on all over the world.

When he finished the glass of water, he rose and went to a dozen boards in sequence, moved the opponents' pieces as they had directed, and then placed his own pieces, ready for the next time messages came in from those particular players. Most of the games were days old; one venerable game had been going on for four months. Dr. Riley suspected that the opponent in that case was a pilot who only caught up on the game when she had a short leave. There would be a flurry of moves for a day or two, then nothing for a fortnight or more.

Dr. Riley settled back into the chair with a sigh of satisfaction. He looked forward to this time of day very much, these moves and countermoves. He rationed himself to one period a day, making himself wait until after his evening walk. During the day he would sneak a look now and then, on the pretense of going to the kitchen for a drink or snack, to see if his computer had received any calls to his game line.

Soon he levered himself from the chair and took a wide briefcase from a closet shelf. In doing so, he jostled a gleaming crown, the one he wore as Chess Master. It was real gold. The goldsmith, who had fashioned everything from a bowl of golden peanuts with precious stones inside to chastity belts and cock rings, didn't bat an eye when Dr. Riley requested a crown to match the one on his favorite chess king. The king was jade, an impractical piece Dorothy had given him on their twenty-fifth anniversary. The goldsmith had simply measured Dr. Riley's head and quoted an outrageous price.

He wasn't going to open the briefcase, but then in a moment of weakness he flipped the latches and raised the lid. Light spilled from the open case, etching shadows more deeply into his lined face. It was a shame that he'd have to give up the crystals for the cause, but he could make more when he had the time. He latched the case and left it by the door so he wouldn't forget it tomorrow. He had an appointment with Burning Rose.

Suddenly he remembered the package he hadn't unwrapped yet. He retrieved it from the kitchen counter and spent the next few hours in his workroom, trying to figure out how he was going to modify the robotic arm he had brought home. It was designed for factory work, but he needed it for his latest doodad, an automatic pet groomer for owners too busy to brush their own dogs. He was playing, letting his productive mind put its feet up and relax with a trivial project.

Sometime after midnight he noticed that he was getting tired, so he went into Dorothy's room to say goodnight.

"Hello, Dottie."

"Working late again, Dear?" Her voice fell softly on his ears.

"Yes, but I'm going to bed now. I just came in to say goodnight. And to wish you a happy birthday."

"Thank you. Sit down and stay a bit. Another year gone by so quickly! It seems like just yesterday you and I were trotting all over the world attending conferences and what not."

Dr. Riley perched on the dainty stool at the dressing

table. When he did not answer right away, silence settled into the room like snow tenderly capping a tombstone.

He had the expensive model, the Sands of Time Mark III, the one with the life-sized image. The Sands of Time series had been a big seller. It was an intelligent holographic device that, once the image of a person at a certain age was fed into it, could produce an image of that person at any age, past or future, with amazing accuracy. Different customers had widely different motivations; police departments and actors perhaps had the most legitimate uses in mind. For others it was vanity or simple curiosity, but the majority of the customers had the same motivation that the inventor himself did: to hold onto a loved one, to somehow spit in the face of death.

Dr. Riley knew, objectively, that Dorothy was gone. He simply chose not to acknowledge it, and the force of that subconscious wish was such that for him, she still lived within this one room. In the rest of his affairs he was coldly analytical. Dorothy's room was simply an untidy corner in an otherwise meticulously ordered mind.

Dottie had been heavily involved in one cause after another, from toxic waste to endangered species. Such things had not been part of his awareness at that time, although he supported Dottie's efforts in a vague way. After she slipped away from him in a room with a lot of equipment and cold, cold floors, he felt that he had to carry on her work. After all, since she spent so much time cooped up in her room now, she couldn't be very effective.

Dr. Riley applied himself to the effectiveness issue and came up with what he thought was an inventive solution.

The first time he had a chance to implement his idea was two years ago, when he attended a conference in Copenhagen. The hotel at which the conference was held was across the street from a park, a pleasant area of woods, trails, and plenty of benches, along with playgrounds and the lilting voices of children at play. A colleague pointed out to him a man who came to the park every day for exercise, to run on the trails. It was a familiar face, one that Dr. Riley recognized as soon as the man had been brought to his attention. Drew Hollings was the man behind a toxic waste spill in Mississippi that had killed dozens outright and damaged the health of hundreds of others in ways that would show up perhaps years later. The crucial documentation that would have proven willful negligence on the part of his company and himself personally conveniently vanished. Lawsuits filed by the injured or their families ended up being settled practically for pocket change. The doctor remembered that Dorothy had been absolutely livid about the outcome. Hadn't it been just the other day that they talked about it?

A plan formed in Dr. Riley's mind, and he acted on it immediately. That afternoon, he took his portable chess set out to the park and set it up on a picnic table near the exercise trails. The cheese was in the mousetrap; all he needed was a mouse. It didn't take long at all before another enthusiast, an older man like himself, joined him and asked for a match. Dr. Riley did not find his opponent to be a challenge, but he said nothing to the man. After all, chess wasn't his purpose for the outing in the park. While effortlessly keeping the game going, he watched for the runner. Hollings showed up on schedule, stopped and sat for a few minutes on a bench not too far from Dr. Riley, and then used the public rest room nearby before moving on.

The next day, Dr. Riley set up his board on a table closer to the rest room. Again his park comrade found him, perhaps emboldened by a loss on Dr. Riley's part that had been intentional. And so it went for three more days, with Hollings keeping the same pattern every day. On the last day of the conference, Dr. Riley slipped a flat black disk into his pocket. It was the size of his palm and had a small strap that looped over one finger to hold the disk in place. It looked for all the world like a joy buzzer, a prankster's standard issue.

When Hollings took his rest break on the bench, Dr. Riley excused himself from the table to visit the rest room. He arrived there ahead of Hollings and removed the disk from his pocket, slipped the strap over his middle finger, and cradled the cool metal in his palm.

A few months ago, he'd invented a gadget that he thought would be useful during surgery. It was no joy buzzer. The disk, when pressed against a person's chest, interrupted the electrical impulses that governed the rhythmic contractions of the heart. In fact, it stopped the heart cleanly and quickly, without fibrillation, cutting off the potentially damaging blood flow through weakened arteries. After surgery, the disk was reversed and pressed against the chest again, stimulating the heartbeat in a less traumatic way than the ordinary shock paddles. Of course, all that was theoretical. Before he got into the thorny problem of testing the device on humans, his lawyer informed him that it was too likely that it would be used for an unintended purpose: murder. Surprised that anyone would think of that use—he hadn't—he suspended the project.

The item neatly fitted into his palm was the prototype, which he took with him when he traveled, for self-defense. It had never been tested. Dr. Riley had once trapped a mouse for that purpose, but when he mentioned it to Dorothy in her room, she was appalled, and that was the end of that.

49

When Hollings entered the rest room, the cramped facility contained only the two of them. Dr. Riley had a brief anxious moment when he couldn't decide whether to let Hollings finish with the reason he came into the rest room in the first place. Feeling that it would be impolite to interrupt, he waited in a stall until Hollings had finished emptying his bladder. He timed the opening of the stall door perfectly, and his hand shot out and thumped the man in the chest. It was over very quickly. Outside, he rejoined the game in progress; his opponent, who was currently in a rough spot, barely acknowledged Dr. Riley's return. When the police came, he was just another old man sunning himself in the park and playing a game of chess to keep his mind active.

He felt the usual thrill he got when an invention proved itself, followed by a little glow of satisfaction that he was carrying on Dottie's work.

"Good night, Dottie," he said.
Immediately the image responded, blowing him a kiss.
"Good night, Dear. Sleep well."

Chapter Seven

After a brutal videoconference, Gunner had his feet up on the desk in his office, relaxing.

"Last appointment of the day coming up," Fran said from the terminal built into the desktop. "You get off easy today."

If Fran thought that today had been easy, she had a chip loose. In fact, the whole week had been frantic. It seemed that every portion of World Power needed his attention all at once. Sometimes he wondered why he bothered to delegate. Things ended up in his lap anyway.

Except Casey Washington. He wouldn't have minded her ending up in his lap, but he hadn't heard from her all week. He didn't know if that was a good sign or a bad one. A spurned journalist could be dangerous. Somehow, though, he thought Casey was about as dangerous as a marshmallow tossed at him from ten meters away. She just didn't have it in her to be tough, as he'd had to be in his rise in the business world.

"Miss Shikuru of Sun Lights, Inc., to see you, Boss," Fran said with a trace of excitement in her computerized voice. "I think you'll get a kick out of this one."

"Send her in. I could use a break. Sun Lights, huh? I hope she's not like that guy who tried to get me to help him patent sunshine."

From time to time World Power acquired small companies with promising products. Gunner usually evaluated them himself, after an initial screening by his computerized trio of assistants. He liked entrepreneurs. He found them refreshing.

Fran informed him that Rose Shikuru had arrived early, which turned out to be a good thing. She had trouble getting through security with her briefcase of samples, and needed the extra time to convince the suspicious staff. Her case was X-rayed, scanned with a Tattletale, and hand-searched. Fran relayed that the guards had been discussing a body search, and that their motivation was suspect. Miss Shikuru was an attractive woman, although not up to Fran's standards of what was good enough for the boss. No woman alive was.

Rose had been ushered into a beautifully decorated private office, one of several waiting rooms where business colleagues were smoothly queued. Each office was fully equipped so that the person waiting could conduct his own routine business. No lost productivity here.

"Please come in, Miss Shikuru," Gunner said. His office was a two-story cylinder with large expanses of curved windows. She stepped tentatively into the room.

Gunner saw a stunning figure of a woman, enveloped in an ankle-length dress of red silk. As she stepped forward, he noticed that the dress was split on one side to enable her to walk freely. Split thigh-high. Her dark eyes rode atop high cheekbones, and her lips matched the color of her dress. In her black shiny hair she had tucked a rose above one ear. She carried a thin black briefcase, and seated herself across from him, the case at her feet. She gazed beyond his shoulder for a moment, seemingly taking in the spectacular view. He was used to it; the effect was predictable. Then she frowned.

"Could we possibly go somewhere . . . darker, Mr. Gunner?" she said.

He wasn't quite sure how to interpret this. Was she

propositioning him? Already? Keeping a straight face, he replied, "Well, there is the washroom. And I suppose if we're going to share it you might as well call me Robert."

At this she smiled. "I think that will do just fine, Robert. Please call me Rose." He led her to the washroom. As he approached, the door slid open, revealing a brightly lit space on a much smaller scale than the main area of the office. They stepped inside and the door whooshed shut behind them. Rose walked over to the countertop and placed her briefcase on it. Then she tilted her hips, stood up on her toes, and eased herself up onto the countertop effortlessly. Seated, she placed the case across her lap.

"Lights off, please," she said.

Bemused, he hit the light button. The room had no windows, and the darkness closed over them. Then there was a glow that grew brighter until it splashed over Rose's seated form, eerily lighting her face from underneath like a Halloween trickster holding a flashlight to his chin. The glow came from the open case on her lap. She reached in and lifted a shining crystal, nestling it in her palm. It sparkled like the facets of a diamond, giving off a warm yellow light. She held it out to him. He took the crystal into his hand, cupping the other hand about it as though protecting a flame from the wind.

The crystal was warm, a pleasant warmth that, combined with the yellow light, made him feel that he was holding a miniature sun in his hand. When he looked up he saw that Rose held out another one in her hand. This one emitted cool, bluish-white light. He took it, and was not surprised at the feel of the crystal. It was like holding a smooth, night-chilled stone. He stood for a moment, one hand blazing with warm sunlight, the other alight with the brightness of a full moon.

"Let's talk," he said.

Over glasses of orange juice in his office—she declined coffee—he listened to her story. Her father, she said, was an incredibly talented but unrecognized inventor. The crystals were his final work before he died about three years ago. No, she did not understand the details of their creation, but she had her father's research journals. Since her father's death, she had been in a fog of sadness. Apparently the fog was now dissipated, blown away by the winds of necessity, and she was ready to promote her father's invention. But she was just a dancer, a member of a struggling troupe that had a lot more enthusiasm than engagements. She didn't have the money or the know-how to go from research notes to marketplace.

"Can these crystals be manufactured larger than palm-sized?" Gunner asked.

"Father wrote that they could be up to a meter across. Theoretically. These are the only two in existence, so I couldn't say for sure."

"How do you see them being used?"

Rose thought for a moment. "Smaller ones as jewelry, certainly. Lighting for romantic dinners. Artificial sunlight for indoor plants. Toys for children. Christmas tree ornaments."

Gunner sat back in his chair and absorbed her suggestions. According to her, two hours of sunlight charged the crystals for a period of ten to twelve days, depending on temperature. One crystalline structure produced light and warmth, the other light without warmth. Up to a meter across. Ideas blossomed in his head. Yes, the crystals could serve all the purposes she described. But there were many more uses—immensely profitable ones, if the manufacturing process wasn't too costly. With cost-effective fusion still elusive, could this be the power source of the New Millenium? His R&D staff would be anxious to get those crystals into the lab, along with Papa's notes.

"Rose, I think it's time for my legal staff to get in touch with yours. If an agreement can be thrashed out, patent rights and so on, I would like Sun Lights, Inc. to work with World Power. No promises, but it could be exciting."

Rose lowered her eyes and seemed flustered. Gunner experienced a sudden stab of protectiveness. She looked young, beautiful, and vulnerable.

"I'm afraid I don't have a legal staff. Sun Lights is just me. I thought it would sound more impressive if I had a company name, so I made one up and registered it. Father always loved his work, but he never cared much about a steady income, you see, and since he died . . ." Rose lifted her eyes and Gunner saw that tears were about to overflow onto her cheeks.

"Things have been difficult. Besides," she said softly, "the crystals aren't patented yet. I thought maybe World Power—you, Robert—would take care of that for me."

An indescribable feeling coursed through Gunner, an electric anticipation, a moment of precognition, a desire to protect this innocent who could so easily be taken advantage of, and would have been, if she'd gone to anyone else with her father's invention. This was more than a business meeting, more than another product, more than another casual alliance with a woman. This woman was special. Could it be that she was going to play a part in his life?

A large part?

He stood and walked around his desk until he was quite close to her. Then he reached out and gently touched the corners of her eyes, drawing the poised tears onto his fingertips. The fragrance of the rose tucked above her ear floated into his face, mingling with her own delicate scent.

"In that case, Rose, why don't we continue the discussion over dinner?"

She nodded and smiled, and his heart leaped.

A large part, indeed.

Chapter Eight

Casey Washington tossed in bed in her Maui apartment and then peered over in the direction of the clock on the nightstand. Her alarm had hands, not glowing digits, so she couldn't see the time. She threw her legs over the edge of the bed, fumbled for the clock, connected, and brought it up to her face. Still couldn't make out the time.

Damn this clock, she thought. Damn, damn, damn!

For a moment she just sat there, wondering how many times she had enacted this exact scene before. It didn't occur to her to get a new clock. Her father had given it to her for her eighth birthday. She had been having trouble getting ready for school on time, and he thought the strident alarm would do the job. Then, as now, if she "just happened" to be sleeping with the pillow on top of her head, she still managed to sleep through the alarm. But there were a couple of unanticipated pleasures: winding the clock, and falling asleep at night to the sound of its regular ticking, a sort of all's-right-with-the-world sound.

She stood up and went to the kitchen, threading her way through the darkened apartment with ease. In the kitchen, she poured herself a glass of mineral water and downed it. She poured another glass and took it out to the balcony her apartment sported. It was barely large enough for two metal mesh chairs. She edged her way between the chairs and sat in one. The metal was damp with night dew, and the cool wetness against her bare skin felt good. She sipped her water, enjoying a breeze that would be stilled by the morning sun, a breeze that carried scents—exotic flowers, ocean breezes—far more enticing than anything that came out of a bottle. It was a clear moonless night. For a time she was absorbed in the grand spectacle of the sky. The stars seemed to her friendlier here below the Tropic of Cancer than they did in more northern latitudes. Warmer, perhaps, like little torches in the sky.

She could see the ocean through the obstruction of the beachfront complexes if she craned her neck up and to the right. When the human-made noises were minimized, as they were at that time of night, she could hear the sound of it, and her imagination easily filled in the rest of the view. She set the empty glass at her feet and closed her eyes. Her breathing slowed and attuned itself to the rhythmic wash of the waves against the beach. Her thoughts floated over the events of recent weeks like a raft bobbing in the waves. Her anger at Robert Gunner had faded somewhat, though she whipped it daily to the level needed to fire her work. It had been a month since Bangkok, a month of frustration, of stalling Kenny, of dead ends. So little was available about the man, and what there was had the stamp of public relations all over it.

After exhausting media archives, she turned to first-hand sources of information: three of Gunner's ex-girlfriends. Tracking them down was easy. Getting them to talk was even easier. The press had made assumptions about the women as vacuous eye candy, and up until now no one had bothered to challenge those assumptions. It turned out that the women were quite articulate. They had no illusions about their role in Gunner's life, and didn't seem to mind it one bit, but they were far from empty-headed. Casey oiled the gears with a little flattery. The interviews were useful in that they postponed the day of reckoning with Kenny at

AmerNet, who was picking up the tabs for the last month's work. The information she got from them was Sunday supplement material. The women inhabited a world constructed to exclude Gunner's business dealings. He was portrayed as considerate and friendly, a real old-fashioned nice guy who would go out of his way to help little children and stray puppies and had in fact done both, even when the media wasn't looking.

When one was digging for dirt, this was not the sort of information that set the pulse racing. The contrast with the cold, calculating businessman of record was infuriating.

One of the women, a redhead with lavish hips and pale green eyes, rated Gunner as "a grade A fuck, maybe A+." Casey felt heat rising in her face, the same physical response that she had experienced in the restaurant with Gunner when the bodyguard had grinned knowingly at her. But the feeling that went with that bodily response was different. In the restaurant it had been pure embarrassment. Now, in the middle of a tropical night, thinking about the interview while sitting nude on her balcony, she couldn't put a name to the feeling. The term jealousy eluded her.

She had heard that Gunner had a new woman in his private digs, a lovely Asian, but her request for an interview with her was turned down cold. Not only did Casey fail to get her foot in the door, there wasn't a glimmer of light leaking out from around the edges of the door. This intrigued Casey, and she began to focus her efforts on getting information about, or preferably directly from, this woman. Irrational? Perhaps. Surely the woman didn't have any more information about Gunner's business doings than the trio of others. Casey felt sure that the article she needed to write, her knock-the-public-on-its-collective-ass article, the brilliant unmasking of the despoiler, had its roots deep in Gunner's mysterious corporate doings.

So deep she couldn't find them.

One thing she knew for sure: it wasn't love that accounted for her behavior. Love was supposed to feel good.

Sometime before dawn Casey slipped from quiet meditation into sleep. She awoke to an abrasive noise, and reached out to shut off the alarm clock. Her groping hand encountered only air, and her eyes flew open. The sound was repeated, and now she recognized it for what it was—a whistle of male appreciation. It was early morning, and the young man—Burt something—whose balcony was adjacent to hers had come out to appraise the new day. In spite of her bareness, and unwilling to let go of the night just yet, Casey stretched languorously, eliciting a whistle in a higher tone. She waved good-naturedly.

Then, unaware of the chair's mesh pattern firmly embedded in the flesh of her posterior, she took herself and her dignity indoors.

Chapter Nine

Willy Parsons was in her late twenties, a rising star in marketing in Superior Services, Inc. She was secretly on the World Power payroll, too, for the last six years, recruited straight out of college as a corporate spy. She was single and attractive. She was salting away the extra money she earned for an early retirement. Very early; she planned to be lolling on some island well before she was forty.

She attended a corporate social event, a weekend retreat at a resort in the Rockies owned by Superior. To her surprise, Harley Bentson, CEO, was there. To her greater surprise, he singled her out and flirted with her. Even though the evening was young, he was already somewhat intoxicated. Sensing an opportunity, she responded shamelessly, even though the man did not in the least appeal to her sexually. She liked her partners young, blond muscle-boy types with raw enthusiasm for the act and plenty of staying power. She went to Bentson's room "for a drink, just the two of us away from all this commotion."

Bentson had not one drink but several, piled swiftly on top of each other. He nibbled on her ear and groped her breasts, then made an attempt to mount her which was thwarted by an uncooperative penis, pale and limp, reminding her of overcooked cannelloni. He fell into a drunken sleep on the sofa. She shrugged, straightened her dress, and prowled the room, sipping champagne. After a full circuit of the room, she came back to an intriguing black leather case on the floor by the television.

It was tempting.

It was unlocked.

Opening the case, Willy found a built-in storage rack containing about fifteen DVDs, with room for twice that many. The shiny disks with their rainbow surfaces rested in slots labeled with women's names followed by a date. Just a year, no month and day.

The old man collects hotflicks, she thought. That's probably the only way he gets off.

She lifted one of the disks at random, the one labeled "Rhonda—1998", and popped it into the player on the side of the television cabinet. She turned the sound off to avoid waking Bentson, although she didn't think there was much chance of that.

Willy's exposure to pornography had been minimal. She had of course seen magazines with provocative pictures of nude men and women. She owned a couple of books acquired during her college days that showed couples doing it in various positions. Very tame. Her inexperience accounted for the fact that it took her almost fifteen minutes to figure out what she was watching. When the realization came, it sent her straight to the bathroom, where she quietly deposited her dinner in the toilet. When she came back out, morbid curiosity caused her to glance at the screen as she reached to turn off the player.

There was a nude woman leaning over a gleaming metal table, the kind that might be found in an operating room. She was bent at the waist, with her legs hanging off the end of the table and her torso on it. The woman was face down, with her upper body fastened tightly to the table with black metal bands and her arms stretched above her head. Her legs were spread wide and tied to the legs of the table. At the point in the table where her breasts fell, there was a gap in the tabletop so that her breasts hung through. A man wearing only a black hood over his face was pressed behind her, thrusting sloppily against her, fucking her from behind.

The wide-angle scene altered abruptly. For a few seconds there was a conventional close-up of the action of the man's penis sliding in and out, then the view shifted again to show the woman's face, which was contorted in a silent scream. Willy was glad that she had turned the sound off. The camera shifted to show the woman's breasts, suspended below the table. Shiny spikes were inserted around each breast, holding them firmly in place. The nipples were missing, neatly sliced off. Below was a device with twin whirling blades. The camera zoomed in to show the blades beginning to rise.

Willy reached out and flicked the switch. Instantly the screen went dark. Her stomach heaved again, but there was nothing left to bring up. She put the disk back into its slot and closed the case. For several moments she debated whether or not to lock the case. If Bentson awoke and found it locked, would he be reassured that his dirty secret was safe? Or would he remember that he had left the case unlocked? If so, and if she locked it, he would know that she had tampered with it.

Take the case and run to the police? Too dangerous. It was clear that to Harley Bentson, a woman's life was a commodity to use and discard. If she tried to involve herself directly, she could conceivably end up with a short and none-too-sweet career as the star of the next flick. There were too many unknowns, too much raw dark fear. She simply left the case as she had found it.

On a table nearby she found some hotel stationery. She folded a piece in half to form a note card and wrote *Harley* in a round, feminine hand on the outside. On the inside she penned *Thanks for the wonderful time,* underlining wonderful with a flourish. She didn't sign it, hoping that Bentson would be fuzzy about the whole incident, including her identity. She propped up the note tent-fashion on the table and left.

"What now?" Willy said.

Gunner looked at her across the desk, trying not to let the incredulity show in his face. He certainly wasn't naïve, but her story caught him by surprise. He'd had lunch with Harley not two weeks ago, sat across the table and smiled at the man. He felt contaminated now.

"First, you give notice at Superior," Gunner said. "We'll hire you, openly this time. The rest you leave to me. If Bentson tries to contact you, let me know right away. My guess is he doesn't even remember who was in the room with him that night."

Willy nodded. "Hopefully I'm below the radar with him. Just another woman he's awed with his sexual prowess."

Gunner spent several days pondering just how to exploit this piece of information about his competitor's vice.

Vice. A crisp, antiseptic word for it. Harley Bentson was a snuff flick aficionado. The real stuff, not the kind faked for the camera. One flick per year, if Willy's report was accurate. The last hours of some woman's life edited into a tidy sixty minutes of rape and highly imaginative torture.

To indulge his twisted sexual appetite, Harley Bentson had consumed one woman's life every year for the past decade and a half, and would continue to do so every year until the Grim Reaper came knocking at his own door.

Give the story to the police and wash his hands of it? Probably, but later. Now it was time for squeezing every possible business advantage from good old Harley.

Chapter Ten

Sarah Grant, head of the Consortium for the Planet, pondered the message from Robert Gunner. He was an enigma to Sarah even after years of working with him. He associated with the Consortium only under conditions of the strictest secrecy. Was he the environmentalist he professed to be in their private communications? Or was his public image the true one—the ultimate exploiter, the megalomaniac beating a path to global disaster with his unstoppable urge for power? These doubts gave all of her interactions with Gunner a certain sizzle, a buzz of danger and excitement.

The phone buzzed, and a little thrill went through her as she reached for it. She'd been expecting his call. His administrative assistant had set it up with hers.

"Sarah, how are you?"

"As well as could be expected." She gestured at her desk, which was crowded with work in progress. The Consortium was an organization with a worldwide perspective and strong financial backing. Most of that financial backing did not come from the grade school classes that held bake sales and car washes to raise money, or fervent clean air proponents who organized protest marches about local industrial offenders. The Consortium didn't turn up its nose at such donations; they mounted up. But the vast bulk of the operating budget came from influential business leaders quietly working for environmentally sane practices.

"What's up?" she said.

"Does something have to be up in order for me to give you a call?"

"If you're flirting, dear, you're about thirty-five years too late," she said with a gentle smile. Gunner knew the smile was not for him, but for her husband Adam, with whom she had just celebrated her thirty-fifth wedding anniversary. "Come to think of it, you were still in diapers then, weren't you?"

Gunner couldn't help smiling. This particular exaggeration was familiar territory.

"Perhaps," he said, "but I was precocious."

She folded her hands on the desk and waited attentively.

"I do have a favor to ask," he said. "A rather large one."

"Let's hear it." She steeled herself. Gunner had never asked her for a favor before.

"I would like you to pass the word to your membership to buy stock in Superior Services. A lot of stock, as fast as possible. Get as high a percentage of ownership as you can, but spread out over a lot of people. No big volume purchases by individuals or businesses. No publicity. Use that tree network you have for your activists."

Her face remained impassive. "What's going on, Robert?"

"I'm going to ask you to operate mostly in the dark on this one, just for the time being." She must have let her exasperation show, because he decided he'd better offer something.

"Ownership of Superior will be changing hands soon. There's a lot more to it than that. I'll meet you at the resort at the end of the next week and tell you the whole story in person. Scout's honor. But I need to get this moving right away." He put on his most convincing, sincere face. "Sarah, it's for a good cause. An honorable cause. Trust me."

Thousands of miles separated them physically, but Sarah knew that Gunner was feeling her eyes on him, and the weight of her judgment. He'd used the word honor twice in fifteen seconds. That wasn't like him. But it was intriguing, and Gunner was a contact worth cultivating.

"I'll do it, Robert, but God only knows what I'll tell the Board. And I certainly hope we're both working under the same definition of honor."

It was late on a Saturday afternoon when Gunner left World Power headquarters off the western coast of Thailand. Due to the time zone difference it was early Friday morning, the day before, by the time he arrived at the Catskill Mountains resort which was the only place he and Sarah Grant met in person. He had taken the helicopter to Bangkok and boarded his private jet. The pilot was assigned a high-altitude polar route. The gleaming high-altitude jet, spare and elegant, arched up and skipped into that ambiguous area between the cold emptiness of space and the cozy blanket of atmosphere. It came down on schedule, looking like a plummeting bird of prey dropping at speed until it leveled out, touched down and coasted to a stop in the center of the target zone on a private landing strip outside New York City.

Reggie Camden disapproved of these spontaneous little jaunts, and had not been above making Gunner wait longer than necessary while he checked and rechecked the jet.

Gunner considered being tweaked by Reggie inconsequential compared to the investment of trust between the two of them. Reggie had come to work for Gunner eight years ago, and since that time a relationship had sprung up, deeper than each man would care to admit. Reggie's previous employer, one Rochelle Quiver, music idol, had slit her wrists while Reggie waited outside her private apartment. He'd been exiled by the erratic woman, who'd claimed she wanted privacy to masturbate. By the time he became alarmed and broke the door down, she had bled to death, neatly and considerately, in her bathtub. Such an event didn't look good on Reggie's work record, but Gunner knew that a bodyguard couldn't protect a person from the devils within. An offer was made and accepted, and Reggie found himself on Gunner's payroll before the corpse was in the ground.

A rented helicopter, with an interior that left much to be desired, ferried them to the landing pad of Forest View Resort. The trip had been made without fanfare, and in fact with considerable behind-the-scenes effort to ensure secrecy. There was no greeting party other than the regular resort staff. Since the Forest View frequently served as a meeting place for celebrities, it offered privacy in addition to the spectacular scenery, both purchased at an outrageous cost. In a short while Gunner and Sarah Grant were seated on a flagstone patio, sipping iced tea, with a cranky Reggie watching from behind closed French doors in her suite.

Gunner told her the story of the discovery of the snuff flicks and what he intended to do about it. She was a good listener. When it was over, Sarah nodded and patted his hand maternally.

"You're doing the right thing," she said. "I'm behind you all the way."

Chapter Eleven

On the long flight back to Headquarters, Reggie relaxed with his boss, trading stories. Sometimes they did that, and usually it was a prelude to some above-and-beyond assignment. Their talk ran in wide circles, and Reggie felt himself tingling with anticipation, but he kept it carefully under control. Gunner would get around to it when he got around to it.

Sooner than Reggie expected, the boss laid out the whole situation with Bentson. He'd always known there was something creepy about that guy. It was in the lines of Bentson's face, and in his moist handshake like wrapping fingers around a salami, and in the way his gaze lingered on a woman like he was slobbering on her head to foot.

"I want you to do something for me," his boss said. "I want copies of those flicks. Draw as much money as you need. Hire a specialist."

A grin sprouted on Reggie's face.

"Boss," he said, "I *am* a specialist."

Which is precisely why the trangun that Reggie carried was illegally modified. It had started life as a conventional tranquilizer weapon, but Reggie rigged it to fire Baby Blues, bright blue armor-penetrating bullets. The term "splattered" was equally applicable to knockout capsules and Baby Blues. The only difference was the degree of permanency. What the boss didn't know wouldn't hurt him—and might keep him, and Reggie, from getting hurt. Sometimes

Reggie thought that the boss must be aware of such necessities and that the "trangun only" ruling was for public consumption. In Reggie's experience, Gunner was no dummy, except maybe when it came to women.

"Kid, your name's Alex, isn't it? You old enough for this?" Reggie spoke to the young man next to him in the van.

"Shit, man, I'm nineteen," Alex answered.

Taking in the young man's clean jaw and boyish eyes, Reggie doubted it. Alex's hair fell over his forehead and into his eyes every time he moved. He had an annoying habit of brushing it back with his thumb, the other fingers outstretched, almost like a salute.

It was a little late now to be working up doubts. Alex was recommended by a source Reggie trusted, and that would have to do.

He and the boy—Reggie couldn't help thinking of him as the boy—were on their way to a dinner party at Harley Bentson's ranch in Texas. But they weren't invited guests. They were part of the extra kitchen help brought in for the evening.

Reggie, who would have been easily recognized by Bentson's security staff, had spent the afternoon applying strips of plastiskin to his face, changing the contours. A little more nose here, a little less jaw. As a playful touch— he enjoyed altering his appearance, it freed something inside him—he gave himself a deep dimple on his chin. Contact lenses turned his Mediterranean blue eyes a dull brown. He applied a black foam-in hair color over his nearly blond hair, and added a few streaks of silver. For completeness he also dyed the hairs on his arms and legs. With a smile that turned up one corner of his mouth, he decided to leave the curly light brown mat at his groin alone.

He slipped the artificial fingerprint wrappers over each finger and thumb, like putting on ten little condoms. A few seconds of heat treatment under a blow dryer sealed the wrappers to his fingers; a special solvent would take them off later. Satisfied with his image in the mirror, he made himself an employee's picture ID, complete with his temporary thumbprint, and slipped it into his wallet, making sure there was nothing else in there that would contradict his new identity. It was an easy preparation, almost a casual job, not nearly as thorough as he had done in other circumstances. But the reports he had gotten indicated that Bentson's bodyguard, Ramon Hernandez, was shamefully lax in checking out the catering help. Tonight was no exception: the catering company hadn't even been asked to provide a list of employees hired within the past month. Hannibal Lechter could get in and amuse himself in the kitchen and nobody would know it.

Ramon's sexual persuasion had rightfully earned him the nickname Black Hole. He didn't seem to mind the nickname.

Alex, unlike Reggie, came by his employee ID card honestly. He had been hired by the caterers a few days ago, and would continue to work for them for another two or three months so that no suspicion would fall on him when the shit hit the fan. He had gotten a higher-than-usual starting salary by dropping his pants, bending over, and accepting the fumbling but tender ministrations of the chief chef, a soft-bellied man in his fifties. Alex was accommodating. Either role was okay with him.

One of Alex's jobs tonight was to unload and set up industrial-sized warming trays from the caterer's van. The other, and far more lucrative one, was to ensure that Ramon Hernandez was looking the other way while Reggie gained entrance to Bentson's rooms.

Reggie hoped the boy was persuasive. He looked at Alex's profile and the way his uniform draped cleanly over a tight belly, and didn't think there was any doubt about that. He just hoped that the Black Hole liked his partners young.

After dessert was served, the kitchen staff was relaxing and snacking on leftover appetizers. Reggie asked the boy to try to give him thirty minutes. Alex looked skeptical. Shaking his head, the boy moved off down the hallway from the dining room to the cavernous party room, where the guests would gather for after-dinner drinks and shallow conversation. The Black Hole had been hovering like a hummingbird over a blooming trumpet vine at the end of the hallway all evening, thereby blocking the stairs to the private quarters. A few minutes later, when Reggie stuck his head out of the doorway, Alex and the Black Hole were nowhere to be seen.

It was crowded in the kitchen. He wouldn't be missed. Reggie made his way up the stairs. The door to Bentson's room barely slowed him down. Neither did the lock on the black case. He opened the lid and briefly checked that all the disks were in place. Reggie unfastened the buttons on his uniform shirt. He pressed both thumbs into spots on either side of his chest, high up near the armpits, and ran his thumbs down hidden seams on his body. A thin artificial chest shell detached itself from shoulders to waist and smoothly pivoted forward. Concealed behind it, in a contoured space between the shell and his real chest, was a storage area neatly divided into compartments. Drops of sweat beaded the golden hairs of his exposed upper body. The chest plate was a handy item, but it was damn hot to wear.

Reggie thumbed open the storage compartment which held a streamlined disk duplicator. He took the first disk from the black case and inserted it, along with a blank one. A minute later he reached for the next disk. Twenty minutes later, the case was locked, the chest plate was back in place, Reggie was back in the kitchen, Alex was five hundred dollars richer, and the Black Hole had once again taken up his position at the end of the hallway.

Before turning the disks over to his boss, Reggie watched one from beginning to end, the same one that Willy Parsons had picked at random. He felt that it was necessary to verify the contents before turning them over. Reggie didn't have a lot of confidence in Willy Parson's inexperienced evaluation. If these were just ordinary porno flicks, or even marginal ones, he was going to destroy his copies. A man was entitled to a little entertainment in the privacy of his bedroom, even if that man was Harley Bentson. Reggie watched with clinical detachment.

He didn't destroy his copies. What's more, he found out something that Willy hadn't reported because she hadn't the stomach to watch the flick to its grisly end. In the final moments the man who was fucking the victim whipped off his black hood and bowed for the camera. It was Bentson himself, in the flesh and considerably red-handed.

Gunner received the duplicate disks with grim satisfaction. He was surprised and genuinely shocked when Reggie related the latest news about Bentson's direct participation, but he saw a tremendous advantage in it. It made his job so much easier. Gunner spent a couple of hours scanning the disks, skipping around, watching segments of each so that he could get a clear idea exactly what kind of bargaining power he had.

He had all the bargaining power he needed and then some.

Chapter Twelve

Reggie Camden wiped his right palm across his thigh, regretting that he was unable to use gloves when he was doing rope work. He usually ended up with a few blisters, but he needed to feel the texture of the cable under his fingers for precise positioning. He eased up on the brake with his left hand and rappelled down another couple of meters. His bare feet touched the brick wall of the hotel and his toes found a mortar crevice easily, controlling his landing. His muscles ached a little and he berated himself for not doing rope work more often.

Well, that's what vacations were for, and this one he'd scheduled months in advance and counted down the days.

It was a moonless night. Reggie's progress down the face of the building was unmarked by the hotel patrons and staff twenty floors below. He paused outside a window on the fifteenth floor and looked around to get his bearings. A puckered scar on his back, below his right shoulder blade, ached with a dull throb. There was no medical reason why the old wound should hurt. It had healed fully some twelve years ago.

Twelve years, he thought. It seems like yesterday.

It had been a memorable day. Reggie, his wife Jeri, and their daughter Tess, long hair flying as she raced about, had spent the afternoon having a picnic. The Rocky Mountains were just about Reggie's favorite place in the world. While Tess dozed on a blanket, made sleepy-eyed by the warm afternoon sun, Reggie and Jeri moved to the edge of the meadow and made slow, sweet love in the fragrant grass. They had been at the cabin almost a week. It was the first time in a long time that he and Jeri had really been able to relax together. His undercover work for the International Drug Counterstrike Force had kept him away from his family for two years, but there was the satisfied feeling of a job well done. Reggie's work led to the arrest and conviction of Cezar Jonvier, a focal point of Malaysian drug traffic. Reggie testified at the trial, and Jonvier was sent to the Barcelona Castle, a romantic name for a decidedly unromantic place: the maximum security institution on a small island off the coast of Spain which housed criminals whose activities were international in scope. Jonvier had been enjoying life, such as it was, in the Castle for about a month before Reggie managed to take some of his accumulated leave time.

In the chill of early evening, Reggie left Jeri and six-year-old Tess trying to cope with lighting a fire in a fireplace with a faulty draw. He hiked a couple of kilometers to the nearest town, jogging part of the way, to buy a bottle of wine and some candles. It seemed to be that kind of evening. When he paid for his supplies at the only store in town, the proprietor asked if the two nice gentlemen, his friends from Barcelona, had found their way to the cabin. Reggie left the wine on the counter and took off at a dead run.

As he rounded the bend in the road, the cabin came into sight. Everything seemed undisturbed, but alarms were clanging in his head and there was an electric tension in the air. His mind registered that Jeri had gotten the fire started. A smudge of smoke from the chimney showed against the sunset, which was now fading to dark. As he ran toward the cabin, the windows bulged oddly, and then the sound and heat of the blast reached him.

It was not enough to level the house. In an instant he knew that the occupants would burn to death, not be killed instantly, unless they had been struck by debris. He continued on toward the cabin, unable to accept that he was too late, prepared to broach the fire to bring his loved ones to safety. He spotted Jeri, silhouetted against the flames, with Tess in her arms. She was trying to reach the window to push Tess out. A cry of pain and frustration reached his ears, but he wasn't sure if it was Jeri's or his own.

As he surged forward, a bullet hit his back, tracing a hot path below his right shoulder and pushing its way through his chest, bringing with it a spray of frothy red from his lung. He pitched forward and rolled, coming to rest with his back against a tree. As his consciousness seeped away, he saw that Jeri hadn't made it to the window.

Afterward he hadn't wanted to live. He fought the healing process for a long time, until the day he realized that Jonvier would be out of prison in twenty-five short years, twelve if he behaved himself.

Three days ago, Jonvier sauntered from the Castle and headed directly for his love nest on the fifteenth floor of the Grandview Hotel in the real Barcelona, not the prison. His woman, a brassy redhead whom he had married by proxy a couple of years ago, had faithfully provided conjugal visits every two weeks. The two had checked in, she giggling, he suave, and hadn't let the maid in for three days. A bodyguard posted in the hallway outside the suite contented himself with magazines and tacos from room service. This evening, Reggie had arranged for room service to deliver a six-pack of beer to the guard, courtesy of his boss. Reggie had no respect for such guards, who gave his profession a bad name. Nor did he trouble himself with the guard's fate when the night's work was discovered.

A slight breeze ruffled his hair as Reggie swung, suspended by cables from the roof, outside the love nest's window. Heavy curtains were pulled tightly shut inside the glass. He drew a laser cutter from his weapons belt and flipped the switch, bringing the pinpoint of ruby light to bear on the window. He set the depth of the laser to score but not cut through. It was a single thick pane with an integral emission-blocking film—easy to work with, that single pane. He scored the surface in a circle a generous meter in diameter. He returned the laser cutter to his belt and removed a trangun. It was not his usual modified weapon. This one felt light, almost insubstantial, in his hand, because it really was a tranquilizer gun. There were two pellets in it. The first was a full dose intended for the woman, the second was a partial dose to disable but not knock out Jonvier. It hadn't occurred to Reggie that he might need more than two shots.

He swung himself out from the building and hit the scored circle on the glass feet first, slapping his left hand down hard on the cable release on his thigh. The glass cascaded into the room, struck the heavy curtain and dropped to the floor. Reggie did the same.

The room was lit with a cozy glow from a single bedside lamp. The redhead sat on the bed, naked, back against the headboard, ass raised on a pillow, knees drawn up. A muffled sound, like a beanbag dropped on a thick carpet, and the first shot from the trangun impacted between her breasts with a puff of blue powder to mark the spot. Her eyes grew wide before she sagged heavily, stunned into unconsciousness by the fast-acting tranquilizer. The second shot left its blue mark on Jonvier's back before he had a chance to raise his head from between her legs.

Reggie moved across the room, bare feet avoiding the broken glass. As he did so, he slipped on a pair of gloves. He checked the door, throwing the privacy bolt, which had been left unfastened. Sloppy. He returned to the bed and hoisted Jonvier up under his armpits, showing no strain with the man's weight. He dumped the slack body into an armchair. Jonvier's eyes were open and he followed Reggie's movements groggily. Removing two short lengths of cord from his belt, Reggie bound the man's wrists to the arms of the chair. He retrieved a piece of clothing, a man's shirt, from the floor, and tossed it onto Jonvier's lap to cover his groin, which glistened with the products of recent sex. The sight bothered Reggie. It made Jonvier look too vulnerable. He pulled the laser cutter from his belt and adjusted the cut for minimal depth. As Jonvier saw Reggie approach with the cutter, a struggle showed in his eyes, but his muscles betrayed him by remaining still. Reggie held the cutter briefly in front of Jonvier's face, then lowered it and made a series of quick cuts in the skin of the man's left forearm. Reggie had noticed the tiny scar of a transmitter recently imbedded under the skin. In an emergency, Jonvier was supposed to slap the transmitter, which would alert the bodyguard. Reggie slipped the tiny disk out from under Jonvier's skin, pocketed it, then turned his attention to the tranquilized woman. He adjusted her on the bed, making sure she wouldn't fall out when her limbs began to thrash later as the drug wore off. He covered her nakedness with the tiger-striped sheets, dabbing thoughtfully at the corner of her mouth where she had been drooling a bit. With her head settled on the pillow, her red hair a fluffy halo, she looked peaceful and quite attractive in repose, almost innocent.

Reggie lowered himself into another armchair and considered what to do next. He was sure that Jonvier had recognized him. The man's eyes, growing more alert minute by minute, showed clearly that he knew his peril. For twelve years, beginning in his hospital bed, Reggie had planned this moment, ending the scenario in various ways, all of which involved the dispatching of this man who had ordered the deaths of Reggie, his wife, and his child. Now that he was here, with the man helpless before him, was the conclusion inevitable? Must he look for personal revenge? Or had he moved beyond the need that had driven him for the last dozen years?

He slipped his hand into a pouch slung across his shoulder and removed a small item wrapped in tissue. It was a hair bow, a delicate pink thing he had bought for Tess. She'd worn it at the picnic. The police had returned it to him with other small personal effects. The edges of the ribbon were singed, but the bow had somehow survived while the owner did not.

The death shrieks of his wife and child, heard on the edge of his own consciousness years ago, played in his mind. With their cries echoing, he levered himself to his feet and moved behind the man's chair, thumbing the controls of the laser cutter. He placed his palm against the man's forehead, tilted his head back, and carved a gap in Jonvier's throat as easily as he had carved a Jack-O-Lantern for his daughter.

He pulled his soaked gloves off and poked them into his pocket for later disposal. Objectively, he checked that he had left no footprints in the blood.

On his way out, he reflected that although he was a weak man, marred and unable to triumph over his baser instincts, he was a happy man.

Chapter Thirteen

The package came when Casey was deep into research on the Internet. She was afraid Kenny was going to cut off her working money, or even demand some or all of it back. The last time she'd spoken to him, his voice seemed strained, but that could be something that had nothing to do with her. She hoped.

She'd answered the door in her bathrobe. The FedEx man gave her the same insincere smile she'd get from the convenience store clerk. There must be someplace that taught that smile. As she signed for the package, she pictured students arriving at Millicent's School for Insincere Smiling, and wondered if they would practice on each other or save the good stuff for the customers.

The package was light and tall, almost half a meter high. She didn't recognize the sender's name, Sun Lights, or the address in Delaware. She decided it wasn't important, probably some kind of sample product. She was on a lot of mailing lists from companies that wanted her to write up their products and obtain free advertising for them. She tossed it on the kitchen table and decided she'd open it when she took her lunch break. The clock was ticking on her Internet connection.

Casey returned to her work. She knew Gunner had that new woman hanging on his arm and wanted information. Nothing had turned up until one of her contacts sent her a grainy long-distance photo of Gunner and the woman getting into a helicopter. The photographer had caught her in an awkward moment, ducking beneath the blades, as everyone seemed to do. She was wearing a bright red outfit and had long dark hair, and that was the extent of what Casey could make out. Her face was obscured by Gunner's shoulder. Casey dubbed her the Red Woman, and it wasn't lost on her that Gunner's hand rested on the Red Woman's hip, perilously close to sliding down onto her ass. A practiced motion, maybe, like the FedEx man's smile.

She glanced at the package on the table. Something about it made her uneasy, tugged at her underneath her awareness of everything else in her apartment. She dismissed it and went on with her work until hunger pulled her away from the computer and into the kitchen.

Casey slapped together a cheese and onion sandwich and poured herself a giant glass of tomato juice. Between bites, she tugged at the wrappings of the package. When she lifted the lid, there was a red silk rose with one green leaf lying on top of some packing material. She picked it up and marveled at it. It was so life-like she expected to see a miniature bee tucked inside the petals. The rose had a pin on the back, so she fastened it to her bathrobe, admiring it against the white terrycloth. It looked like a rose blooming in the snow. Who would send her such a beautiful object? She dug into the packing peanuts, thinking that whoever sent it, it wasn't an eco-aware company or they would have used biodegradable packing.

Then she had the contents out on her table. A child's doll, in pieces, the severed head painted all around with red to resemble blood. Casey's heart raced as she stared at the horrid thing. For just a moment, a terrible moment that would be with her the rest of her life, she'd thought the doll was a real baby. The skin was cool and pliant, and the hair that her fingers had grasped was fine and soft, where it wasn't matted with paint. What really got her were the eyes. They were wide open, blue, and had red tears painted in the corners and down the rounded baby cheeks. Bloody tears.

Casey swept the doll's torso and head back into the box and crammed the lid on it. It was a long time before she could put her thoughts together enough to call the police. Longer still before she realized that the doll had been wearing a dress with initials childishly embroidered on the front. Her initials.

By the time she remembered to take the silk rose off her bathrobe, the police were already gone. She pitched it out the window.

Chapter Fourteen

Vowing to get rid of those excess ten pounds for the sixth time in as many minutes, the otherwise slender man with the soft spot around the middle sucked in his stomach. He sat down on a convenient outcropping, wiped the grime from his forehead with the back of his hand, and shone the carbide light on his helmet onto his watch. The timepiece, its familiar weight a comfort on his left wrist, delivered the bad news: he had less than thirty minutes to make it to the Glow Room on time. He pressed on, acquiring a couple more scrapes on his already throbbing knuckles.

Muttering to himself that the effort was getting to be too much for his middle-aged body, he made the last rope descent. He lowered himself onto the formation Papa always called The Throne, and switched off his carbide light. Settling in, he allowed himself a sigh. Except for the time he spent in the Army and a few years afterwards when he lived in Europe, he had been in this place on this night of the year for as far back as he could remember. The magic remained as strong as it was thirty-five years ago when Papa first took him under Polecat Hill. The last time he was here with Papa, his father made him promise to come back here every year.

While he waited for his eyes to adjust to the underground darkness after turning off the lamp, he fingered the clunky wristwatch, feeling the deep gouge in the crystal that was a reminder of his last trip into this cave. The hand-scratched inscription on the back, *To Elvis on his tent birthday, Love Papa*, wove itself into his thoughts. The misspelling of tenth was characteristic of everything his father did: good intentions aplenty, marred by minor flaws. Or major ones, as in the case of marrying Mama.

Papa Callahan was a farmer in Tennessee, with a prosperous family homestead handed down to him reluctantly, because Papa was the only one of five sons who showed any willingness to work the land. The reluctance came from the fact that things just seemed to happen to Papa. Things like cutting the hay a few days too late because he went camping instead, or letting one of the feeder pigs stay on as a freeloader because he liked the particular way its tail corkscrewed. The farm never completely failed, just kind of ambled along, never prospering either.

Mama was a plain woman whose life turned sour for some reason Elvis never understood, and Papa, if he knew, never explained. Alcohol eased her premature passage from the world when her sons were only six and four years old. When he was old enough to put two and two together, Elvis realized that Mama and Papa had only been married five years when she died, not long enough for his entry into the world under the blessings of marital ties. Not only that, but Elvis didn't look a whole lot like Papa, certainly not the way his younger brother Presley did, with his dark good looks. No one would mistake Elvis for good-looking. There was a wildness in him, in his eyes and the way his legs acted as if there were springs in his ankles and the way his hair spilled over his collar. During the summer, when his stringy body was as brown as an acorn, and he was bare-chested and barefoot, Papa would call him a native. He wondered, even then, a native of what land, for surely it wasn't Tennessee.

Papa did his best to raise his motherless boys, but there were a lot of skinned knees that went unkissed and a lot of birthday cakes that never got baked. When he came of age, Elvis joined the Army like his namesake. Presley took off for the good life on the West Coast and wrote to Papa, one page with words spread out to eat up the space, about every six months.

In the Army, an aptitude test channeled Elvis into the design of explosive devices, and suddenly he knew what he wanted to do with the rest of his life. He approached his work with respect and awe and the same boyish enthusiasm he reserved for the swimming hole on the first day of summer vacation. He eagerly learned all the Army could or would teach him, and when he got out he found a mentor. For five years he lived in Portugal with an octogenarian whose overindulgence in wine and women was almost as legendary as his reputation within the tight circle of explosives experts worldwide. When the man died in the arms of a teenage village girl, Elvis went back to the farm.

He moved into his old bedroom on the second floor, and Papa welcomed him back in his quiet way. Elvis helped with the animals and the planting and the harvest, and in his spare time he began working on remodeling an old shed down by the creek. After a while, when the shielding went up over the windows, he began to lock the shed so that Papa wouldn't blunder into it and blow the farm, and himself, to bits. He told Papa that he was going to have a business on the side, a sort of customized tool shop. Papa got into the swing of things, greeting male clients with a handshake, his calloused hand engulfing the customer's. Female clients got a nod of his head and a slight tipping of his sweat-stained cap.

Things began to change around the farm after Elvis had been in business for a time. A new tractor replaced the one that kicked like a mule. The farmhouse hummed with a climate control system that eased Papa's arthritis. One spring, Elvis suggested that Papa let the fields rest for a year or so. Freed from his labors, Papa spent a lot of time walking in the woods that summer, and the next spring it was even easier to let the planting slide. A few summers after that, Papa didn't come home from his walk one evening. Elvis found him dead in the woods, sitting on the ground with his back propped up against a tree. In his lap was the treasure he had been admiring, the skull of some small animal scoured to pristine whiteness by time and scavengers.

Elvis stayed on, letting the farm go back to nature. He sent his brother money every year on his birthday, just as Papa had. The shed grew into a solid affair with a copter pad on the roof. He greeted clients in his modest reception area, served them lemonade or hot chocolate according to the season, and listened to their stories. He insisted on conducting business face-to-face. When a client finished talking, he would either agree to take on the project or politely decline. Nothing that was said ever passed beyond the shed in the Tennessee countryside, whether he accepted the project or not. He expected honesty from his clients and gave it freely in return.

The local law enforcement establishment had word from the highest authority that Elvis's farm and the people who came and went were not subjects for idle curiosity. The military and other less well-known branches of government, his own and those of other countries, were represented on his client list.

Elvis had a clear code of ethics concerning his work. The end result of his immensely satisfying creative process was an explosive device usually used for destroying some inanimate object, but sometimes used for assassination. Early on he established a few simple guidelines. He wouldn't work with a client whose target, if human, was under twenty-one years old. Until word got around about that particular guideline, he was getting requests almost weekly from wealthy parents wishing to dispose of inconvenient teenage sons or daughters. The target had to be an individual; no mass carnage scenes, please. He never worked both sides of a situation. He held himself free to decline, without explanation, whether the reason was technical infeasibility or the color of the suit the client was wearing or annoyance because his bran cereal wasn't working. And he never, ever, got involved in marital disputes. The fee for one of his devices was a minimum of a quarter of a million dollars, and as far as he was concerned, there wasn't any maximum.

Every now and then he did what he thought of as charity work, because a job particularly needed doing.

Then came a turning point in Elvis's life, and it came about because a client lied to him. Elias Crawford, a senator from Oregon, approached him and asked for help in dealing with a cult leader who had indoctrinated Crawford's daughter with spiritualistic jargon. The cultist defrauded the family of millions of dollars, every penny the girl could get her hands on. Crawford had eventually gotten his daughter back by arranging to have her kidnapped and deprogrammed. He said that he wanted to spare other parents the heartbreak of having their children used in this manner, but his efforts at prosecution never got off the ground because the cult maintained a thoroughly respectable front. The documentation Crawford produced was compelling. There were grainy photographs of his white-robed daughter taken right after her kidnapping, records of her psychological treatment, and finally a recent recording she had sent to her father expressing her regret at having become involved with the cult.

Elvis took it all in and made a favorable decision. He told the senator to come back in two weeks with the payment. Actually, he had decided during the senator's explanation exactly which product he was going to use; it was already nestled, snug and deadly, in an isolation chamber inside the shed not ten meters from where they were sitting. But the roof was leaking on the old farmhouse and he needed a couple of weeks to strip off the three courses of shingles and tack on new ones before winter, and it didn't bother him in the least to make the senator wait.

It was a sensational weapon, the latest in an exciting new phase of his work—miniature explosives with biological delivery systems. He had taken a bomb half the size of his little fingernail and broken it down into microscopic parts, each with a specific shape and magnetic alignment that would make it fit back into place like a puzzle piece. The parts were then encapsulated within a sheath of frog's intestine that sufficiently interfered with their magnetic attraction so that they were inert. Suspended in an odorless and tasteless liquid medium, the fragmented bomb could be easily ingested in a drink. Once inside the victim's body, the fragments made their way into the bloodstream and dispersed throughout the body. White blood cells, the body's cleanup crew, obligingly devoured the sheaths surrounding the fragments as soon as they were recognized as foreign tissue. The fragments themselves were impervious to the action of the white blood cells.

The body's blood returns over and over again to the heart. Whenever a microscopic fragment passed through the heart, carried there by the pulsing river of the victim's own blood, it would click into place on the growing shape of the bomb. If a fragment wasn't close enough to the growing mass for the magnetic attraction to draw it into position,

perhaps on the next pass through the heart, or the one after
that, it would be. When the bomb was completely formed,
in a day or a week, it would seek freedom the only way it
knew how: by blasting its way outward through the yielding
flesh of its prison. A tightly controlled directional blast, of
course, nothing excessive. No use hurting any bystanders.

Elvis rated it a bit on the messy side but elegant nevertheless. With a touch of his morbid humor, he code-named
the product Heart Attract. The senator's target was the in-
augural usage, and Elvis scanned the news eagerly for days
after the delivery, waiting for news of the cult leader's
death. What he spotted instead greatly disturbed him. An
activist who had organized opposition to a major commercial development within the senator's state was reported
killed by a mysterious bomb blast. Approval for the development, which environmentalists claimed would push a
couple of endangered species over the edge to extinction,
was rushed through during the short period of confusion
following the activist's death.

A phone call to the right person produced a copy of the
autopsy report within an hour. It didn't take Elvis long to
recognize his own handiwork, and when he did he was
angry in a cold, dangerous way. This was clearly a wrongful
death, an application not sanctioned by Elvis, and one that
he would have rejected if his client had been honest. The
death itself was an unfortunate thing that weighed upon his
mind, but the betrayal of his trust was paramount. Over the
winter his conviction grew that he could not stand passively
by and let this betrayal go unpunished.

He had a hunch the senator would be back, and sure
enough, when the lilacs bloomed that spring, the man sat
smugly in his reception area telling another tale of woe. As
Elvis freshened Crawford's lemonade with additional ice

cubes, he smiled and nodded as he plunked a special cube into the glass. He agreed to the new request and asked Crawford to return the next day with the payment. Luckily for Elvis, the senator's white blood cells were sluggish enough so that the cash was in hand before the senator developed heartburn on a massive scale.

When the special investigators who were working the senator's death followed the trail to Elvis's farm, the investigation came to an abrupt halt. As explained to the commander of the operation, it was like following bear tracks to a cave, with tracks going in and none coming out. You know damn well the bear's in the cave, and only a fool would poke his head in and shout. Instead of disturbing this particular very valuable bear, the department's damage control staff put in some long hours creatively redirecting the public's attention.

As he studied the senator's autopsy report, complete with clinically harsh photographs, Elvis felt something stir inside him. For the second time in his life (the first time being when he took the aptitude test that landed him in explosives work), he felt a push that moved him in a new direction. At first it was hard to admit, but he reasoned that any sane person would have difficulty acknowledging such a thing about himself. Once he let go of the clinging notion of social unacceptability, it was easier.

He had found it pleasant to use such an elegant device personally rather than through others, and he wanted to do it again. He had ample opportunity as Wrongful Death, a member of The Six. He thought his costume, a rendition of the aftermath of his signature Heart Attract device, inexplicably beautiful.

As Elvis sat on The Throne in the Glow Room, surrounded by the eerie phosphorescence of subterranean fungi, he lifted his eyes to the small hole in the roof of the chamber. A crescent moon, a pale sliver with slender arms wide in anticipation, eased into view in the cylindrical shaft that penetrated to the surface. Elvis, scraped knuckles forgotten, pupils wide to gather in the light, renewed his promise to Papa.

Chapter Fifteen

"Two notations from Fran, one code TLC, and one code TOPBIZ just coming in," Sally said. "Can I listen in, Boss?"

"Prioritize in order as TLC, Fran, TOPBIZ," Gunner said to his computerized personal secretary. "No, you can't listen in. Weren't you a redhead before lunch?"

"That's a question a man should never ask a woman, especially a blonde. Playing code TLC, confirming no audit." Sally pouted.

From a device atop the monitor in Gunner's private helicopter, a beam of light shot out and formed into a holographic image about fifteen centimeters high, suspended over the desk. There was no sound. The three-dimensional image began to move. It was a woman riding bareback along a deserted beach, the horse splashing its hooves at the water line. She was wearing a red halter top and skimpy, high-cut red shorts. Her long pale legs pressed against the shining black sides of the horse. Breasts bounced in time with the horse's gallop. She leaned forward over the horse's neck as if she were sharing a secret with the magnificent animal. The horse came to a stop, spraying sand, and she slid off.

Gunner held out his hand, and the image seemed to step into his palm. She faced him, smiling, and blew him a kiss. Moments later the halter top and shorts lay in the sand. Then she began to dance in place, feet spread, rotating her hips in little circles. The nude woman gyrated in Gunner's palm, then lowered herself to the sun-warmed sand, lying full length in his outstretched hand. The image faded.

Gunner let out his breath in an explosive gasp. The whole message had lasted three minutes or so, and he felt like he had been holding his breath the entire time. He sucked in air noisily and replayed the fantasy in his mind before speaking.

"File that one under Recreation, Private, title Beach. Indefinite retention."

"I live to serve, Boss, but that's a nix on the indefinite retention. The message is coded with a ten-day fadeout. Fran is next up."

The communications from his appointment secretary were brief and all business, and he answered in a similar way.

"Fran says thanks for the feedback. Final message, code TOPBIZ, engaging decryption . . . Message ready. Absenting myself now, Boss."

Sally disappeared from the screen and was replaced by a woman seated at a desk in nondescript surroundings. It was Sarah Grant of the Consortium for the Planet.

"Hi, Robert. I'm sorry I missed you. Fran says you're at lunch." The woman leaned forward. Her silver hair framed her face beautifully and somehow made her brown eyes seem even more compelling. "I would have preferred to give you the news in person, but here goes: We've reached the twenty-five percent level." Her eyes flicked downward for a moment, as though she was checking something out of his view. "Make that twenty-six percent. The membership has been responsive." Her eyes bored into him. She spoke softly. "Go for it, Robert. Good luck."

It was good to have her confirmation, but he'd been keeping close tabs on the stock purchases himself. Gunner had already sent one of the duplicate snuff flicks to Bentson via courier. He addressed it to Bentson, with "Open by Addressee Only" emblazoned on the outside. He took no care to cover the point of origin of the package. Inside Gunner placed the disk and a slip of paper with his own private phone number on it, which Bentson would surely recognize. He alerted Reggie to take steps to increase security, only to find that Reggie had already done so. Then there was nothing to do but wait.

Worldwide courier service was provided by Bentson's own company, Superior Services, and it provided well for its own. Delivery was speedy. Colleen, his administrative assistant (or the Ad Ass, as she liked to refer to herself), asked him if he would take a call from Bentson.

"Sure, put the old goat on," Gunner answered. "No audit, please."

"Boss, why do I get the impression that you live a secret life? I know, I know, I'm going . . ."

Colleen's image faded from the screen and was replaced by Bentson's. He was seated at a desk with puffy white Texas clouds ambling across a blue sky visible in the large expanse of glass behind him. He didn't say anything for a moment, just drew deeply on an impressive cigar. The top of the desk was clear except for the package Gunner had sent. Bentson made unwavering eye contact, electronically at least.

"Long time no see, Harley," said Gunner. "How's the world treating you?"

"Cut the bullshit, Gunner, and let's get to it. Are your communications secure?"

Gunner glanced down at the scrambler light, glowing solidly. Bentson should know that the conversation was shielded. Why would he bother to ask? Nervousness, probably.

"Yes, we're secure."

"What is the meaning of this package you sent?"

"I'd have thought the meaning was obvious." Gunner favored the man with an innocuous smile. It came easily to him, which said a lot about his mood at the moment.

"So I'm being blackmailed. What kind of money are we talking about here?"

Gunner allowed his face to form a parody of indignation. "Really, Harley, the 'b' word should be left to lawyers and the police." He sat back in his chair and studied Bentson's face. The man's lips were pressed tightly together and his brow was deeply furrowed. Occasionally a muscle twitched below his left eye that caused the jowl on that side of his face to shake. Like a bowlful of jelly. "Let's just say that you and I are going to come to a new business understanding."

"Like what?" A flash of relief had been briefly visible on Bentson's face before it was replaced with a negotiating mask.

"Like you're going to sell me enough of your personal horde of stock to make up twenty-five percent of the total ownership. Then you, personally, are going to enjoy an early retirement."

There was silence as Bentson smoked and considered. No doubt he was wondering why Gunner wasn't asking for a controlling interest right off the bat. How could Gunner expect to accomplish anything if he left Bentson as a majority stockholder? If Bentson sold twenty-five percent ownership, it still left him with twenty-six percent out of his current fifty-one. Even if he retired formally he still would wield tremendous power. And there was nothing in the stated deal to prevent him from gradually building back up his percentage via stock purchases on the open market. Bentson puffed a delicate smoke ring, and Gunner could practically see the mental smoke drifting away as the plan became clear. Obviously there was a connection with the puzzling and worrisome stock turnover of past weeks. Purchases of a hundred shares or a thousand, all small potatoes.

He found himself wishing that Bentson would turn down the offer. Watching those disks had put Gunner in a distinctly confrontational frame of mind: preferably now and preferably physical. The muscles of his shoulders and thighs tensed and a skittishness tickled the base of his spine. When Bentson's answer came it was a disappointment to the warrior inside Gunner.

"Sell at what discount?"

As soon as the dealing was done, Reggie would slip some incriminating evidence into an envelope and send it off to Interpol. Bentson wouldn't get to enjoy his retirement for long.

Chapter Sixteen

The helicopter dipped gracefully to the roof of the World Power, Inc. headquarters. A light rain had begun during the flight, so a covered walkway was extended from the roof dome. Gunner remained seated until Reggie pulled the door open. The two of them walked in, leaving the pilot to his own devices. There was a lounge under the dome where a pilot could be reached twenty-four hours a day. Gunner's four pilots were free to work out their on-call hours among themselves, as long as they kept the Ad Ass informed.

Headquarters was located on a large tract occupying the western half of Phi Phi Don Island. The island was just off the western coast of the Thai mainland, adjacent to the narrow leg of land that flares out into Malaysia. It was shaped like a capital letter "H." Expensive resorts occupied the eastern upright of the "H." Private thatch-roofed huts with every amenity, rich wives and mistresses baring their bodies to the tropical sun on white sand beaches. The western upright housed Gunner's HQ complex. The horizontal bar in between was the site of the original village, still occupied by fishermen who took their boats out into the bays sheltered by the uprights. Access to the HQ complex was strictly controlled, but otherwise the corporation enjoyed congenial relationships with its neighbors.

Gunner took the private elevator. It zipped down toward the residential floor. Annoying elevator-type music filled the compartment until Gunner reached out and stabbed the mute button.

"Some things never change," he said to Reggie.

Reggie grinned. "Yes, sir, and that can be a good thing. Take women for instance."

Gunner wondered, as he had before, what motivated a person to choose a livelihood as a bodyguard. Reggie was intelligent; he certainly wasn't all muscle and no brain. From outward appearances, he could have been an executive or a scientist. He was compact and quick, not musclebound. Years ago he had taken a bullet meant for Gunner, surviving only with the best high-tech medical care that money could buy. There was a scar from sternum to groin on that tight-as-a-wire body.

On his back was a second scar, one that preceded the chest wound by several years. The circumstances of that one had been in Reggie's file when Gunner hired him. Once a special agent of the International Drug Counterstrike Force, Reggie had snared a key figure in the Malaysian syndicate after a couple of years of undercover work. The man's hot anger reached out from his prison cell and scorched Reggie's beautiful wife and six-year-old daughter. Reggie couldn't stop the carnage; he stopped a slug instead. The vicious attack really left two scars, one that puckered the skin below his right shoulder blade and one in his heart. Gunner didn't think any less of Reggie, even knowing that the man carried around a shitload of resentment.

Gunner had noted with interest that the Malaysian Big Shot was killed within a few days of getting out of prison, throat slit by an unidentified assailant. He would have brought the news item to Reggie's attention, except that Reggie had taken a short vacation at about that time. By the time Reggie got back from vacation, and Gunner got a look at him smiling and relaxed, the whole thing seemed a dead issue.

So did the man have hobbies? Friends? Lovers? The rare moments of Reggie's life that belonged to him alone were just that: private. Every day he used his physical presence and his knowledge of security procedures to shield Gunner from over-eager media representatives, competitors with big plans for a future without Robert Gunner blocking the way, fanatics with real or imagined grudges, or just plain nut cases. Gunner would like to think that some personal quality of his own inspired such loyalty. On his more cynical days he thought that the salary Reggie earned had something to do with it.

Reggie was number two on the World Power payroll, second only to Gunner, with a bonus structure that would turn his corporate heads green with envy if they knew about it. Why pay some corporate president who sits on his brains all day more than a man with scars like that? If Reggie had been stashing even a percentage of that salary away for the past few years, by now he could buy and sell those corporate presidents. And that was fine with Gunner. It was a matter of priorities, and to Gunner surviving was high on his list. Especially now. Especially because of her.

The elevator opened in the reception area of Gunner's suite. Reggie watched until the door closed behind Gunner and then, presumably, entered his own apartment across the hall. Reggie never accompanied his boss into the suite when there was a female in residence, which was a lot of the time. Gunner knew that Reggie considered that a sloppy practice, but the bodyguard's presence was inhibiting. Not to Gunner, to the women.

Gunner felt his business cares drop away as the door closed behind him. His life was highly compartmentalized, and this slice of time belonged to him and Rose. There was a conference later this afternoon, but he had three hours free. Deliciously free. He slipped off his jacket, dropped it on a bench by the door and headed for the garden on the balcony.

It was cool and dim in the suite, just the way she liked it. Double doors opened to a large climate-controlled dome brimming with plants, mostly roses. Out there it was warmer, and tropical-strength sunlight poured in through the glass overhead, its warmth tamed by the special coating on the glass.

She was kneeling in a heavily mulched bed, snipping blooms past their prime. Hearing him enter the dome, she got smoothly to her feet and faced him. She was wearing the red outfit, the halter and shorts from the beach fantasy. He stepped toward her and held out his arms. She fitted herself into them, and he buried his face in her hair.

"Rose . . ."

She pulled away to arm's length. "Did you like my holo? I had a lot of fun making it."

"Without me?"

"I was thinking of you. That's what made it fun." Her lips, as red as the halter and shorts, puckered below dark eyes as she blew him a kiss. As he watched, she unfastened the halter, and pushed the shorts down over her hips and let them drop. For a moment he just drank in the sight. Then he bent to trace the rose painted between her breasts with the tip of his tongue. She was wonderfully salty from her exertions in the garden.

She laughed. "I'm so hot and sweaty—I must taste terrible! How about sharing a bath? Want to scrub me clean all over?" She moved close and began to unbutton his shirt. He slid his hands down her back and cupped her ass. A trickle of sweat slid over his fingers.

"Afterward," he said.

★ ★ ★ ★ ★

Gunner sank into the bubbling hot water up to his chest. The chilly air of the suite made for a sensual contrast. Above chest height he was pleasantly cool; below, his love-spent body luxuriated in the warmth. Rose had just gotten out of the whirling water, goose bumps rising as cool air washed over her. Her delicate wet footprints trailed her receding backside. She hurried over to a lounge chaise, one that was fully reclined, almost horizontal. She draped herself face down, fitting her body into the chair's smooth contours just as she had so recently fitted that body against him. Warm air burst from the thousands of tiny jets on the surface of the chair, drying and massaging her all over.

Sighing, she turned over, with no trace of self-consciousness about her nudity, folded her arms behind her head and closed her eyes. In a few moments, Gunner saw her upper abdomen rising and falling in a slow sleep rhythm. Some part of his mind remembered that Reggie had told him women breathe differently from men. When asleep, a man's ribcage will rise and fall, but the place that rises and falls for a woman is below the ribcage. When feigning sleep, the pattern tended to reverse. Reggie was full of little facts like that. Gunner wondered if that particular fact had ever come in handy.

Thinking about feigning sleep brought Casey to mind. She was probably the type who pretended to be asleep so she wouldn't have to relate to the man afterward. She was beautiful in a wholesome sort of way, though. Gunner had experienced a nagging feeling of disappointment after their abrupt parting. During their light conversation, he had gotten the feeling that there could have been something more there. Perhaps a glimmer of friendship, a rare commodity in his stratified circles. There had been a lot of other women in Gunner's life, but only one other who was truly a friend.

Friend, lover, wife—all those roles had rested easily on her slim shoulders. It was an early marriage, she all of twenty-one and he a worldly and wise twenty-seven. She died before their first anniversary in a senseless—weren't they all?—car crash. Only a few days before the crash they had found out that they were to be parents. She was on her way to join him for a celebration. In the fifteen years since her death, Gunner had been through innumerable one-nighters and a series of lengthier relationships. The relationships were all superficial ones, conveniences for business entertaining. Sometimes it was necessary to show up at social functions with a beautiful woman on his arm, dazzlingly dressed and with a suitably adoring expression on her face. There was never a shortage of such women, who were content to share, however briefly, in the ultra-rich lifestyle that was part of his public image.

It's different with Rose, he thought. Different from the start.

He adjusted a water jet against that tricky spot in his back, the place that tensed up before public appearances, and let memories rise to the surface of his mind like the bubbles in the warm water.

His reverie was disturbed by the hourly chime of an antique grandfather clock. Gunner stepped out of the tub and wrapped himself in a thick robe. Rose still napped on the lounge chair nearby. Feet slapping against the tiled floor, he left the room and went into an adjacent office area. There was something he needed to do that couldn't wait.

Gunner swiveled in his chair and looked out the window. He poured a glass of wine. The relaxation he'd felt with Rose had slipped away at the prospect of the phone call ahead. With a sigh, he turned back to his desk and tapped into the computer a code only a handful of people in the world knew.

The call was answered immediately. Gunner wondered momentarily if the man on the other end ever slept. The screen showed a neutral-looking office with traditional furniture and no windows. Behind the desk was a figure cloaked in the cone-shaped distortion of a state-of-the-art communications privacy field. The cone originated at the ceiling and spread out to completely cover the person. Its surface was black and non-reflective, showing no pattern at all. It was so cohesive it appeared to be a solid surface, but Gunner knew a person could step through it without harm. It tingled a bit, that was all. Gunner was not using a privacy field. He could have, but to do so would be viewed as somewhat impolite, since he was the caller. Impolite was not the impression he wished to make. A wavering voice spoke to him, intentionally distorted to make identification by voice analysis more difficult.

"Robert, isn't it? It's been a long time."

"It has, Godfather."

There was a pause. Gunner let the pause develop fully, but the silence was not an uncomfortable one.

"We are both busy men," the voice said. "Proceed."

"I wish to ask a favor," Gunner said. The small knot in his throat tightened. He sipped his wine.

"The scales are tipped because of what you have done for me. We can balance them now, if you wish."

Gunner relaxed a little. So far, so good, he thought. But you never know with this man.

"It has come to my attention that a certain upcoming sporting event will result in an upset victory for the challenger."

"Indeed. If you intend to profit from this knowledge, I have no objection. That is hardly in the nature of a favor."

"I want the champion to win. To retain his title."

Once again there was a pause. This time the level of discomfort was substantially higher.

"You ask much. Can you tell me why this is important to you?"

"I'm going to have the information leaked to a competitor of mine, one who will bet heavily. More heavily than he can afford. And that is exactly the position I want him in."

"I see." Silence filled the room. Gunner forced himself to sip his wine, knowing that the person behind the privacy shield was scrutinizing him.

"The debt I owe you is a significant one. I can deny you nothing that is within my power to provide. But you should know that making this change causes me certain difficulties. A few business associates of mine are already invested in this venture," the voice said.

"There is more," Gunner said. When there was no reply, Gunner continued. "My competitor's bet may be substantial. I want to arrange to have it accepted even though it may be well beyond your usual limits. I'll take the loss myself. When my competitor is unable to meet his obligation, I would like your . . . collection agency to motivate him." A smile flitted across Gunner's face. "I'll be waiting to charge to the rescue."

"It is done. With one exception: I must be allowed to take the loss personally, whatever it may be."

Gunner nodded. "The scales are even. If I may, I will still count you as a friend."

In answer, the figure shifted beneath the privacy field until the head and shoulders were visible. It was an eerie effect, the visible portion of the body floating above the black cone, sliced brutally at the boundary. The face was distinctive, a handsome man of indeterminate age. The most striking feature was the serenity evident in the eyes and the slightly upturned corners of the mouth. An arm extended from beneath the cone of darkness, holding a wine glass. The deep red glow of the wine within the sparkling crystal goblet drew Gunner's eyes. Long afterwards, when he tried to remember the face, his mind summoned up only the wine glass. Perhaps that was for the best.

"Come, a toast," said the man. It was the voice of a confident man, a man who was long past the need to flaunt the raw power of his position. Gunner picked up the glass of wine on his desk and raised his arm to clink glasses, symbolically at least, as the man continued speaking.

"A toast to friendship. To champions. To granddaughters. Most especially to granddaughters."

Both glasses were drained.

"How is Veronica these days?" Gunner asked. He remembered her, so light in his arms, a blur of curly dark hair and tears, lots of tears, as he carried her from the burning building. Left behind in the building were the girl's kidnappers. When the word had reached him that the Godfather's only granddaughter had been kidnapped, Gunner had thrown his own considerable resources into the search. His contacts paid off, and it earned him the man's gratitude. When he began the search, it was a calculated thing, an effort to ingratiate himself with a powerful man. But the satisfaction he felt when he placed that terrified girl in her mother's arms went far beyond his calculation.

Gunner had more in common with Reggie than the bodyguard probably knew.

"She's well. Safe and happy, thanks to you. Her birthday party was last month. Already she is nine years old. Soon she will be married and I will be a great-grandfather. You should marry, Robert. Have a family. It is the way of things."

Gunner smiled. He had been thinking along those lines himself.

"I'll consider it," he answered, but the screen was already dark.

Gunner pulled open a side drawer of his desk and removed a wooden chest about the size of his hand. It was a jewelry box, highly polished, with a small key inserted in the lock. Turning the key, he lifted the lid and gazed at the inscription inside.

On a silver plate, in flowing script, was engraved *To my darling Liza, on our first anniversary, the first of many to come.* He had ordered it one morning, smiling and joking with the clerk, telling anyone and everyone about his impending fatherhood.

It was the morning of the crash. When the box arrived several days later from the jewelry shop, he discarded it angrily. In the middle of an anguished, sleepless night he retrieved it, tearfully put a few mementos into it, and put it into the desk that had belonged to his father. For several years it lay there, corner chipped from the impact when it was first thrown out, until he was ready to open it and go through the contents. Some pictures, a gold locket with a few strands of hair, his and hers, curled together contentedly. A love letter, the only thing he had left in her hand. He sat silently with the lid open for several minutes, then locked it and put the chest back into the desk drawer. He stood up, taking with him a small box that had been on the desktop for the last three weeks, and went back to the spa room.

He woke Rose with a hand on her shoulder. She

stretched with an easy grace and smiled at him. He opened the gift box, which held a glittering diamond ring. For a moment he thought that her eyes glittered from deep within, a strange, cold, disquieting light, as cold as the heart of the diamond. Not the sort of woman he or perhaps anyone could honestly call a friend. That just wasn't part of their relationship. He knew it and he felt he could live with that.

He would have to live with it. He couldn't live without her.

Then the moment passed and he held out the ring box.

"Rose, will you marry me?"

She slipped the diamond on her finger, put her arms around his neck and kissed him. He found himself thinking about how she had to sell her body in the bleak time after her father died, something she had only recently admitted to him. After the kiss he held her and whispered fiercely into her ear.

"You're safe now. No other man will have you."

Chapter Seventeen

After Gunner left the suite, Rose pulled on her barely-there swimsuit and wrapped herself in a cotton cover-up. She sat in her own study, at a small, uncluttered desk with a glass top and marble legs. On the desktop was a voice recorder. She drew a blank tape from a desk drawer and put it into the recorder. She leaned back in her chair and composed her thoughts before speaking.

"To rest of The Six: Greetings from Burning Rose. I have much to report. Phase I of Project Crystal has been accomplished—penetration is complete." She paused, thinking wryly that with Gunner, that was a fair statement.

"Thank you, Chess Master, for your pretty crystals. Gunner's scientists have a new toy, and have not yet found out about the manufacturing problems. It was a great way to get a foot in the door. Gunner went for the helpless act, although it galls me to play the role. I am living in his private suite at HQ. He even set up a rose garden for me, the dear." She twisted her wrist to catch the light with the spectacular diamond on her finger.

Strange. Diamonds are formed with tremendous pressure and heat but have such cold, cold hearts.

She shied away from the comparison—her observation about diamonds could apply equally to herself.

"Whatever background check they did on me should be complete by now. The fact that I'm still here I owe to your talents, Cold-Blooded Serpent. My records must have been very convincing. There's a bodyguard here that doesn't like me," she sniffed as though such a thing were inconceivable, "and I'm sure he would have cheerfully turned me out if he had anything at all to justify it to his boss. Speaking of the bodyguard, I have an urgent request. Wrongful Death, I must have—must have—a microbomb which cannot be detected by a Tattletale. The last time we spoke, you thought you could make one that could only be picked up during the last thirty seconds before exploding. That presents difficulties. With the reflexes that guard has, it might as well be thirty minutes. But I'll take it if you can't come up with anything better." She put in the jibe deliberately. Wrongful Death was a touchy soul. A little derision might spur him to greater inventiveness.

"It is especially sweet that Gunner is taking this romance business seriously. He proposed marriage today. Gave me a ring that should finance a project or two after he's out of the picture. I'll be traveling to Rio with him in a few weeks, and then into the interior, for the ribbon cutting on the construction of the dam. I need the supplies before then." She paused for a few moments, long enough for the recorder to go into standby mode. When she continued her voice was low, causing the device to boost its pickup.

"I just want all of you to know that I appreciate working with you. I could never do anything this ambitious, this fulfilling . . . without your backing. You're like family to me."

Rose removed the tape and placed it into a pocket in the bottom half of her swimsuit. Already inside were a few coins. She picked up a canvas bag with her swimming supplies and slid her feet into a pair of sandals. She clack-clacked her way to the rooftop dome, fastening her cover wrap as she went. The helicopter was waiting when she got there. She could get used to that kind of attention.

The pilot touched down on the pad at the beach, and

Rose bounced lightly out, beach bag over her shoulder. She waved.

"Two hours, Mahomet," she said, raising her voice to be heard over the whirling rotors. She held up two fingers in case she wasn't heard. The pilot nodded and returned a thumbs-up before taking off. She knew Mahomet desired her, caressed her with his eyes whenever he got the chance to do so without being too obvious. For his benefit she dumped her bag in the hot sand, tossed the wrap aside and bent over. Her back to the departing copter, she pretended to be searching for shells in the sand. Gratifyingly, the pilot hovered overhead considerably longer than necessary to make the turn back to the complex.

She had asked to be taken to the fishermen's beach, not the private stretch of glistening sand inside the complex. She had done this before, on the pretext that the shelling was better there. Actually, it was better, and she passed a few pleasant moments as the sand yielded its latest treasures. She held them up to the sun, admiring the intricate curves and other-worldly colors before stowing them in the canvas sack she brought for that purpose. Then she moved closer to the ocean, until the waves gently pushed sand over her toes on the rush inward and pulled it back on the flow outward. She stood for a few moments, watching the small fishing boats riding the gentle swells in the sheltered bay and drawing the sea smell deep into her lungs.

Backing up a few steps, she spread her towel and unfolded her sunscreen umbrella. From a small package, the umbrella popped open at the touch of a button into a spacious shelter that arched protectively over her like the curl of a wave. She was not a sun soaker, one of those who indiscriminately exposed her skin to unfiltered ultraviolet rays. Even the dome of the rose garden filtered harmful rays. Underneath the umbrella, she carefully rubbed a waterproof sunblock lotion over the exposed portions of her body. Then she ran down to the water, waded in up to her waist, and began to swim with powerful, practiced strokes.

Further out than most swimmers would attempt to go, she stopped to rest at one of the fishing boats, clinging to the side briefly and chatting with the occupant in fluent Thai. After catching her breath, she opened the pocket at her waist and tossed a couple of coins into the bottom of the boat. It was a touristy thing to do. Angling off to the right, she headed for another boat. At this one she also chatted with the fisherman, then tossed a handful of shiny objects into the boat. Among them was the tape containing the voice recording she'd made. Then she headed back to the beach, coming ashore quite far from her towel. She strolled leisurely, keeping to the wet portion of the sand scoured by the waves in deference to her bare feet. When she reached her towel, it was nearly sunset. She sat cross-legged under the umbrella, wishing that she had something cool to drink. Or anything at all to drink. It had been a strenuous swim, even by her standards.

She pushed the discomfort of thirst and protesting muscles from her mind and reviewed the afternoon's events. The diamond flashed on her finger, and she wondered if the salt water would damage it somehow. She didn't think so, but it would be better to take it off when swimming from now on. At least, as long as it was necessary to wear it.

No other man will have you.

Rose's lips twisted as the words echoed in her mind. Old thoughts pushed persistently at her awareness, like the waves stroking the sand. For a while she tried to stem the tide. Finally she closed her eyes and gave herself over to the past, which swarmed up into her consciousness like a black cloud.

111

Chapter Eighteen

Adam Grant kissed his wife's cheek and smoothed back her hair in a gesture that was a decades-old comfort between the two of them.

"Sarah, you're so distant. Is there anything you'd like to talk about?"

Sarah sighed. He could see that she was enjoying the rhythmic stroking of her hair, her forehead, and closed eyelids. It was early morning, and she was lying beside him in bed. Often they talked quietly at the beginning of the day. It was their special time before she went to the office and he went to the far corners of the Earth. Adam was a nature photographer, one of the best. Sometimes he was gone on assignment for weeks at a time; occasionally he just assigned himself to do something he particularly wanted to do. In a way it kept their relationship fresh. When he came back after three months in Tegucigalpa or Kathmandu they made love with the passionate abandon of strangers.

"I'm just having a rough time at work," Sarah said. "I've been making some very important decisions, working with a new partner, based on hunches. I could turn out to be the world's biggest fool." She discussed details of her work with her husband only rarely, but when she did so, she seemed to value his input.

"Not a chance of that, my dear," Adam answered. "When have your hunches been wrong before?"

"They haven't. Especially when I proposed to you."

"You see? Whatever it is, I have confidence in you."

"Let's talk about it tonight," she said. "I'd like to get your reading on it."

His hand strayed downward to her throat and then to her bare breasts. "I'd be glad to, but I can't tonight. I have a show opening in London. I thought you knew." He leaned over her and tenderly kissed one nipple and then the other.

"I remember now. Congratulations, by the way. You go ahead and have a good time. This problem will keep until you get back."

His answer was wordless but very expressive.

After a quick shower, Sarah dressed and walked to work. Adam waved to her as she left. They lived in an old farmhouse in a two-hundred-acre valley at the northernmost end of the Appalachian Mountains in Pennsylvania. There was a separate building on the property, reached by a meandering brick path, where Sarah worked most days. When it was necessary, she took a copter into Washington, D.C., to the Consortium for the Planet headquarters. But most of her work was done from her home office overlooking the duck pond.

After Sarah left, Adam called for airport transportation. As he waited to be picked up, he packed quickly and efficiently. The morning flight from Washington to London was overbooked as usual. Adam hated crowded flights and he hated airline food. He munched a candy bar while breakfast was served to those around him gullible enough to accept their trays.

After disembarking and clearing Customs, where there was the usual fuss over the photographic equipment he carried everywhere and refused to allow to be X-rayed, Adam went to a utilitarian area of the airport. Moving confidently and casually, he picked up a small suitcase from a pay

113

locker and left. He went directly to his hotel, sharing a public limo with three other travelers.

In the hotel room, he ordered lunch from room service, tossed his clothes on the bed, and stepped into the shower. When he came out, he found that lunch had arrived. He pulled on his boxers, sat on the edge of the bed, and ate his lunch from the cart. He was hungry; the candy bar had long since worn off. He ate quickly because of hunger and also because he didn't have any time to waste.

After the last bite of pie—Key Lime, his favorite—he opened the suitcase he had picked up from the airport locker and began to dress himself with the contents. A purple shirt with ballooning sleeves, bright yellow oversized trousers, suspenders in a black and white checkered pattern. He drew the rainbow wig over his steel gray hair, wondering exactly when his hair had changed to gray. At sixty-three years old, he still felt as vigorous as he could ever remember feeling. He took a makeup kit from the suitcase and went into the bathroom to use the mirror. When he came back out, his face was painted white with exaggerated red eyebrows and lips. On his cheek was a large black painted teardrop with a diamond glittering in the center. He pulled a red bulb nose from the suitcase and fastened it on.

He drew on white gloves, feeling the little button shape embedded in the fabric covering the tip of his right index finger. When squeezed just so, as in a hearty handshake, the button ruptured outward with a burst of air, pushing its contents through the fabric and through the top layer of skin of the person on the other end of the handshake. Adam's own finger was protected by a special inner lining of the glove. It was just like getting a compressed air vaccination.

In this case, the vaccination would not prevent a deadly

disease. It would start one. The Jericho-B virus was fast acting and there was no effective antiviral agent. It was a product of the biological warfare genetic research done in the last decade by countries that took the trend toward worldwide nuclear disarmament as a personal insult.

Jericho-B was not easily passed from an infected person to those the person came into contact with during his brief remaining time on Earth. It was not a weapon of mass destruction. It was an assassin's tool, a pinpoint killer. All stock of Jericho-B was supposed to have been destroyed—launched on a collision course with the sun, cleansed by fire. Most of it really was aboard that drone capsule. Frontier Enterprises had held back some and auctioned it to the highest bidder.

The Six had deep pockets, and it had acquired the virus. It seemed appropriate to put it to use against the individual responsible for the clandestine sale of such a deadly substance in the first place, a man who clearly knew he was selling an item with no purpose but murder. A small but deadly portion of the remaining stock was embedded in the button hidden inside the glove.

Tearful Clown was ready to go to work.

The target was Emil Koldabi, CEO of Frontier Enterprises, Inc. He was in London today for the dedication of a new wing of a children's hospital that had been mostly funded by Frontier. A good cause, yes. But it was purely public relations for the company, part of the diversionary effort to draw the public's interest away from a project on the drawing board, which was strip-mining the moon. Adam intended to do something about that in the most direct manner possible.

The person most likely to achieve the CEO position after Koldabi was out of the picture was a woman named

Marlena Rosten. Research by The Six had revealed that she was much more moderate, possibly even pro-Green, or at least pale green around the edges. But she was currently overshadowed by Koldabi, to the point that her programs were not enacted, her rational influence not felt. It was believed that Koldabi tolerated her within the organization because he planned to bed her; after that, she would be looking for another position besides working under the boss. The lady had proved to be resistant thus far, which further heated Emil's ardor.

In approximately forty-eight hours his ardor would cool considerably, along with the rest of him.

A family with young children waylaid Tearful Clown on his way out of the hotel lobby. He smiled, made animal shapes from balloons that he pulled from his voluminous pockets, and let the children toot his rubber nose. He took a taxi to the hospital complex. When he got there, it was easy to mingle with the other clowns. There were about a dozen of them, invited to pose with young patients for the cameras, to look colorful and add to the well-planned gala atmosphere.

When Koldabi came through, Tearful Clown contrived to be holding a very appealing little girl in a hospital gown in his arms. The ring of reporters passed near and asked Koldabi to pose with the clown and the girl. Excellent material for the Life Style sections of a dozen newspapers. Tearful Clown saw Emil glance at the man next to him, who must have been his bodyguard. The man nodded. The bodyguard edged himself just far enough away to be out of the picture. The clown held the girl up to Emil so she could give him a kiss on the cheek. He steadied himself with a hand on Emil's shoulder. It was his right hand, and it was pressed just hard enough. Then the media swarm moved on to the reception inside. Tearful Clown returned the little girl to her room, leaving her with a bouquet of flowers pulled from his sleeve.

The one-man photography show was a success that evening, with Adam Grant wearing black tie and a smile like a cat who has taken a couple of chomps out of a mouse and knows it can't run too far.

Chapter Nineteen

When Adam Grant was twenty-eight years old, he felt the future stretching out before him like a golden ribbon. Vietnam was behind him, he had his journalism degree, and he was in love. Sarah!

The wedding was large and pretentious, a concession to Sarah's parents, who were still trying to come to grips with their daughter's choice for the groom. Both newlyweds wanted children right away, but the months slipped by and before they knew it, two years had passed with no results. Finally bringing themselves to the point of medical intervention, they found out after the first visit that Adam was sterile. They decided to use artificial insemination. Sarah caught a set of twins on the first attempt.

Adam loved the twins deeply, and was a wonderful father to his son and daughter, but he was never able to express to Sarah that he had a lingering sadness that he wasn't their biological father as well. The twins' birthdays had a special meaning to him, a juxtaposition of joy and sadness exemplified by the sad-faced clown costume he wore at their birthday parties.

Several years later he attended a reunion of his Vietnam buddies. He almost didn't go. It was a bittersweet thing to see the living, the walking reminders of the ones who didn't come home. Sarah practically pushed him out the door, and far into the night he raised a glass to her wisdom as he traded stories with his friends. He brought home a piece of information that profoundly disturbed him. He wasn't the only one who was sterile. In fact, almost half of those who had been willing to talk about it were unable to father children.

He had not, to his knowledge, worked with or been exposed to Agent Orange, nor had any of his fellows. No one showed any of the other debilitating effects of the defoliant. Yet it was almost impossible to dismiss as coincidence.

The demands of fatherhood and a rapidly advancing career as a photojournalist nearly swept the mystery from his mind. The addition of photography to his work had come about when an editor asked him if he could submit a few relevant photos with his next piece. The medium excited Adam, and he felt that at some point in his life he would probably drop the journalistic aspect of his career and move into photography exclusively, probably wildlife or landscape work. A year later, when he was doing a joint investigative article with another veteran, the mystery bobbed to the surface. This time he grabbed on, and exploiting the contacts he had made in his short but intense career, he began trying to uncover the facts.

There were so many dead ends, so many doors slamming in his face, literally and otherwise, that a less persistent man would have given up. But Adam's residual sadness, so at odds with the rest of his fulfilling life, drove him on.

In the dim interior of a bar in a neighborhood of Washington, D.C., not the kind of place where power lunches were held, he got what he believed to be the true story from a paid informant. A disillusioned and bitter career military man, the informant wandered widely from the core of the story. Adam continually prodded him back to it.

An outside party had developed a chemical in secret. The informant, despite considerable pressure from Adam, would not or could not reveal the developers. It caused male sterility with minimal additional effect. The outside party sold the chemical to both sides in the conflict. However, both sides refrained from using it, not out of good will, but because the other side would gain a terrific public relations advantage that would probably outweigh the psychological deterrent value of the biological weapon. Stalemate. Finally a misguided patriot in the U.S. Army chain of command hatched a scheme to use the weapon against a small portion of his own troops, blaming it on the enemy, of course. The news would then break that the Godless Commies had used a hideous weapon, and worldwide outrage was sure to follow.

A single helicopter sprayed the chemical over the sleeping soldiers. Those who were not out on patrol that night woke up in the morning with a fever and damage to their sperm-manufacturing capability. The fever departed in a day or two. The true damage came to light, for most, years later.

The plot came to nothing in the end. Before the disclosure could reasonably be made, the dramatic airlift from Saigon intervened. Victory, however shallow or false, was in. Worldwide outrage was out.

For the price of another beer, Adam bought the name of the true believer who originated the idea.

There was one thing the Army had taught him well, and that was how to kill. Adam found that, like riding a bicycle, it was a skill that didn't fade with time.

At his twins' next birthday party, he added something to his clown outfit: a sparkling tear. He wasn't sure whether it symbolized his original betrayal in the steamy fields of Vietnam or the more recent loss of innocence on his part, a loosening of the restraints of civilization that had enabled him to strangle the man in his bed. But he thought he could feel that teardrop poised on his cheek long after he had put away his costume.

Chapter Twenty

Gambling had been a part of Carlos Angeles' life as far back as he could remember, and probably before that. He liked to have the odds in his favor, but he preferred it when the teeming masses did not realize that the odds were in his favor.

In other words, he liked to cheat.

There had been ample opportunity to exercise his tendency to cheat during his rise to become head of GlobeCom, Inc. But that was simply business. It was in his personal life that gambling had grown to encompass more and more of his daily activities. His long-suffering wife played along tolerantly when he cajoled her into making bets on ordinary things such as what color socks he would pull from a drawer with his eyes closed or what the high temperature would be in Zurich or Manila. She did not realize that by playing along she was reinforcing his compulsion. She would have been surprised to discover that her husband cheated even in these small circumstances, that the odds were slanted in his favor enough to almost, but not quite, guarantee a win. That was part of the delicious excitement; that slim possibility of losing. Carlos did not delve into the deeply buried reasons for the betting and the cheating: the need to come out on top, the need to be in control. He only knew that it made him feel good to win, so win he did, as often as possible.

Today he was going to place the biggest bet of his life.

A week ago, he had gone to lunch with a business colleague, a woman who owned a small company that supplied GlobeCom with a patented fiber optic cable terminator. GlobeCom's headquarters were in Berlin, and the woman was in town attending a convention. She was in a holiday mood, more cheerful and intimate than she had ever been during their prior business negotiations. At first, Carlos thought that she was trying to seduce him. Then he realized that she was simply unwinding, and he had never seen her in an unwound state. The conversation had been bouncing rapidly from topic to topic and then it got around to sports.

He was surprised to discover that she was a kick-boxing fan like himself. Not many women were. During the main course, she said that the upcoming championship match was rigged to be an upset. The current champion, a seasoned athlete with an extremely impressive record, was going to lose to an upstart challenger.

Keeping his voice and facial expressions under what he hoped were iron control, Carlos had questioned her in a seemingly casual manner concerning the source of this information. Her niece was married to a man in the family business, as she called it. As she chatted, it dawned on Carlos that the woman had ties to organized crime.

Throughout the rest of the lunch, Carlos' head buzzed with more than just the wine.

This could be it. His chance to make a killing, to hit it big. A sure thing.

It was like a litany he recited to himself, excitement growing. He could barely contain himself long enough to finish the lunch gracefully. Back in his office, he checked out the woman's story as well as he could. He got in touch with an underworld contact and gave him the name of the niece's husband. The response was that the man was "way, way up there." That's all it took for Carlos' compulsion to begin to eat at him. He checked the odds for the match and found that they were thirty-to-one against the challenger. Thirty-to-one! A fortune could be made. More than that, there was the thrill of betting against the odds and coming out on top.

By the next morning, Carlos no longer thought in terms of if he should bet, but simply how much. A hundred thousand? Paltry. A million? Not enough for a sure thing. For days he worried over the amount. Each day the bet grew both in monetary and emotional significance. At last he settled on an astonishing figure, worthy of the once-in-a-lifetime opportunity. Fifty million dollars. After the match he would be a billionaire, and then some.

There was only one small problem. Carlos didn't have that much.

In the past Carlos had done many things that stretched the meaning of accepted business ethics. He had his own set of rules, which restrained him from outright murder, but pretty much left him free to operate short of that. He had "borrowed" money from GlobeCom before to take advantage of personal opportunities that had to be pinned down immediately, not next month when he might be able to come up with the cash legitimately. But he'd never played with the books for straight gambling. And never on this grand a scale. But, he told himself, the entire transaction would be invisible. There would be no need to actually draw the funds. It was like a short-term highly leveraged deal, all on paper with no actual movement of cash.

After all, this was a sure thing.

Carlos Angeles, billionaire. He liked the sound of that.

A little voice at the back of his mind worried about that sure thing business. Was this information truly reliable? Why had the woman passed this information along? She shouldn't have told anyone. If she was a real gambler, she would know that spreading information like that would eventually result in the odds being lowered, as bets poured in. She wasn't a real gambler, though. She didn't know the value of the information.

The decision seemed to make itself, and Carlos was just along for the ride. He placed the call.

Leisure Enterprises. Please enter your customer ID and security code.

Carlos typed slowly, thick fingers striking the keys deliberately. Practically the only time he used basic level on a phone was to place a bet. He entered his code name and password.

Thank you, Sunflower. Please choose your event.

A menu was displayed. Carlos punched in the number next to the kick-boxing championship match.

Champion or challenger?

He put an "X" next to challenger. His breath came fast and shallow.

Odds thirty-to-one against. Less than one hour to event, odds locked. Bets will be confirmed. Enter amount, please.

His fingers trembled as he hit the keys. The numbers glowed on the screen as he added zero after zero. Fifty million dollars. They looked good, all those zeroes.

There was a slight pause.

Bet exceeds limit. Please confirm amount, Sunflower, and request excess liability authorization by entering your personal code again.

Carlos did as requested. This time the pause was longer. It seemed very long indeed.

Bet confirmed, amount $50,000,000 U.S., position challenger, odds thirty-to-one. A bold move, Sunflower. Confirmation number follows. Please record the number for your reference.

Carlos fumbled for a pen and copied the string of numbers on the back of one of his own business cards.

Thank you for playing, Sunflower. Enjoy the match.

There. It was done. It couldn't be undone. There was no backing out after a confirmation number had been issued.

Carlos assembled a small group of fellow enthusiasts in the entertainment room in his home and paid a large premium to view the fight. The room was lavish even by a videophile's standards. Several groupings of chairs faced a two-meter wide screen, which was mounted on the wall like a large painting. The picture was sharp, bright, and created a strong impression that the events on the screen were happening in the same room with the viewers. The sound system was the latest equipment, a custom configuration that complemented the volume and shape of the room.

There was considerable talk and good-natured bantering among those assembled during the pre-broadcast announcements. Carlos was thrilled deep inside, but outwardly he was calm. No one else in the room knew about his bet, of course. It was enough that he knew.

The boxers, on their knees in the ring, faced each other and bowed. When they rose, the action was lively and the first two-minute round was neutral, neither side accumulating an overbearing point advantage. Traditionally it was a playful round, the one performed with the visual appeal of a choreographed dance. The boxers celebrated their sport in a sincere display of physical prowess. In the remaining rounds, they got serious. During the second and third, Carlos wondered when the challenger would begin to shine. The score favored the champion, although not overwhelmingly at this point. Points were scored with every blow that landed, by bare foot, knee, elbow, or fist. The boxers rarely used their padded gloves, unlike the Western version of boxing, with its reliance on brain-damaging punches.

When the tenth round was over, and the running point scores displayed throughout the match flashed up as confirmed by the officials, Carlos put his head into his hands and wept. The guests drifted out, subdued and puzzled by his reaction. Carlos was not a drinking man, but that night he accepted the gift of oblivion.

In the morning, he fumbled in his medicine cabinet for something to help him erase the effects of the previous night's indulgence. The phone chimed. He went to answer it, then thought better of it. Sitting on the edge of the bed, trying not to disturb his still-sleeping wife, he let the answering program take the call while he listened in.

"Mister . . . Angels, is it? Mister Angels, this is the Collections Director of Leisure Enterprises. The account number you have on file with us contains insufficient funds to cover your recent loss. You have until two o'clock today to correct the situation. Have a nice day."

Carlos squeezed his eyes shut against the pounding in his head. He went back into the bathroom for a glass of water and downed a headache pill.

"That's Angeles," he said, "not Angels." Momentarily he wondered how Leisure Enterprises knew his name and home phone code. Gambling customers were anonymous and used code names. Apparently anonymity vanished in the shadow of a fifty-million-dollar debt.

He got through the morning meal somehow, avoiding his wife's eyes and her efforts to converse with him, and escaped to his office. He had a suite of rooms on the top floor of a renovated red brick building in what had been East Berlin prior to the reunification. He notified his secretary program that all appointments for the day were to be rescheduled. She threw up her hands, gave him an obscene gesture, and began making calls.

A few minutes of checking with his personal accounting software confirmed his rough estimate. The Angeles family fortune, if it was abruptly liquidated with the attendant loss that involved, amounted to about ten million. Given more time to raise the money he could realize perhaps twelve million, at most thirteen with sympathetic or inexperienced buyers. As head of GlobeCom, he should have accumulated a vast fortune. But gambling had bled it off steadily.

He needed forty million dollars more by two o'clock—not the sort of problem he could solve at the local pawnshop. He thought about taking the ten million and trying to parlay it. Hope stirred, and Carlos considered where to start. Horse racing, maybe. He'd had better than average luck there. But in a few short hours? No way. And what if the horses were against him today? Reluctantly he began issuing the instructions to liquidate half of his personal holdings, directing the proceeds to the Leisure Enterprises account.

Five million will hold them. I need more time to deal with this.

Hours later, with the deadline come and gone, a small package arrived for Carlos. Inside was a video. Puzzled, he played it.

When his wife Maria appeared on the screen, he began to get a sick feeling. Why would someone send him a video of his wife leaving her surprise birthday party? He'd known that the lunch date with a friend was actually a party for her. He'd been planning to attend, until the events of the last few hours had driven the thought from his head.

Maria's bodyguard, who was also her driver, brought the limo to the curb and stepped out to help her with the load of birthday presents. A car came around the corner fast, too fast. The windows on the side next to the curb were open, and as the car passed the limo, gunfire erupted, spraying the limo. The driver swept Maria's feet out from under her, knocking her to the ground, scattering the contents of the gift boxes. Carlos saw what at first seemed to be puffs of dust approaching his wife's head. Mesmerized, unable to look anywhere else, he watched as the puffs neared.

There was no sound. The dust danced in silence. Craters formed in the concrete as chunks lifted themselves out of the sidewalk and vanished, like divots on a golf course.

Abruptly Maria was kicked, hard, as the bodyguard's legs uncoiled like a powerful spring, impacting her chest and sliding her roughly along the sidewalk a short distance. Then there was a splatter of red onto the gift boxes, her birthday presents. The bodyguard, left leg shattered into a bloody tangle of bone and muscle from the knee down, drew his gun from beneath his jacket and rolled onto his stomach. He steadied himself with both elbows, took a deep breath and held it, then squeezed off a single shot at the receding car. Carlos saw the rear windshield soundlessly explode into a million rainbows glittering in the morning sun, but the car kept on going.

But for the heroics of the bodyguard, it might have been a clean hit.

"My wife's injuries are minor," Carlos Angeles said. He leaned forward earnestly in the chair and placed a finger tentatively on Gunner's desk. "A couple of broken ribs, bruises, abrasions from the sidewalk. The driver lost a leg, but he'll be all right. My wife's scared, Gunner, and so am I."

Gunner leaned forward, resting his elbows on the desk. He knew all of these details, plus a couple that Carlos did not know. There had been no intention of harming Maria Angeles, or the guard, for that matter. The shots were only a warning meant to motivate Carlos. Had the guard not interfered, there would have been no injuries. But there had been a real casualty this afternoon. The single shot that the bodyguard had fired shattered both the rear window of the receding car and the skull of its passenger. Legs could be replaced with constructs of metal, plastic, and computer chips; heads could not. The victim had been a distant relative of the Godfather. Gunner had expressed his regrets to the man earlier. The response had been a shrug and chilling remarks about the nature of the business and the thinning out of over-exuberant young employees.

"An interesting story, Carlos," he said. "What do you expect me to do about it?"

Carlos pulled himself up straight in the chair. "Can't you guess? I'm asking for a loan."

"Why me? Why not one of the other corporate heads? They can afford it."

Carlos shook his head. "They'd use this opportunity to ruin me personally and take over GlobeCom. But I will go to them if I have to. If you turn me down."

"So you think that I won't ruin you? Or take away your company? To what do I owe this confidence?"

"You're an honorable man," Carlos said. He raised his eyes and locked them with Gunner's. Neither man said anything for some time. "Also, there will be concessions," Carlos said with a sigh.

Gunner wondered what Carlos would think if he knew that Gunner had set up the whole situation in the first place. There was no time for such questions now. They were the stuff of sleepless nights, curled against Rose.

"Yes, concessions," said Gunner. "I won't ruin you. Entirely." As he spoke Gunner experienced a heady feeling. His plans were moving along well, pieces clicking into shape like a global jigsaw puzzle.

Carlos sat back, weighing the meaning. Then he nodded. Gunner swiveled the phone on his desk to face Carlos.

"Call your betting service," Gunner said.

"What, here?"

A glare from Gunner set the man's fingers working. He tapped in the number, then his ID and code as requested.

Sunflower, your account has been referred to Collections. Your privileges are restricted. Payments cheerfully accepted.

The screen showed a Leisure Enterprises logo and a balance due of forty-five million. The half of his personal fortune that Carlos had liquidated had been credited, but it didn't make much of a dent in the debt. Gunner reached out and turned the screen back toward him. He typed in an account number of his own next to the balance. It was a showy gesture. He knew no funds would be drawn from his account. The Godfather may be a cold bastard but he was a reliable one when it came to settling debts. A few moments passed in silence.

Thank you, Sunflower, for your prompt consideration in this matter. Full privileges have been restored. How about trying your luck? There are some exciting camel races today.

Gunner laughed out loud, startling Carlos, and turned the screen back so that Carlos could see the response. A faint smile tested the corners of Carlos's mouth.

Is he actually considering placing more bets?

"Cancel your membership," Gunner said.

Carlos looked stricken.

"Concession number one. Cancel. Quit. Cut the strings. Now. After all, I can't keep bailing you out. I can't afford it," Gunner said, "and neither can you. Financially. Professionally. Emotionally. Also, I want you to get therapy and join Gamblers Anonymous. Keep in mind that I'll find out if you slip."

"It's come to this. I'll do it," Carlos said. He looked at the screen, his eyes lingering for a moment on the tantalizing *try your luck* and the zero balance of his debt. He made menu selections that closed his account with Leisure Enterprises. After he entered the final confirmation, he leaned back in the chair.

Sorry to lose you as a customer, Sunflower. We hope your association with Leisure Enterprises has been a pleasant one. We would appreciate it if you would recommend us to all your friends.

"Concession number two. Three-fourths of your remaining personal funds will be donated to a charity of my choice. I choose the Consortium for the Planet. Pay up within the week."

Carlos sighed, but a smile was working its way onto his face.

"I will be a poor but happy man," he said. "You surprise me. Since when have you become Green?"

"You're not the only one in for a few surprises, Carlos. In fact, your entire corporation is going to see you in a whole new light. Now about concession number three . . ."

Thirty minutes later, the men shook hands and parted. At his desk, Gunner decided he was beginning to like Carlos Angeles. The man was struggling against an undesirable behavior, but he had good qualities too. Gunner felt that he could work with him, and that Carlos would honor their agreement to the letter. Perhaps Carlos would even enter into the spirit of the agreement sometime in the future.

Gunner sat at his desk for a time. His thoughts roamed,

but eventually turned to Harley Bentson, to lives wasted, to the dreams and hopes of parents for their daughters, and the cruel dashing of hopes for some of those parents.

"Colleen, get me Interpol," Gunner said.

An image formed on the computer screen of a modestly attractive woman, the type you might find behind the desk in the library.

"Interpol? Really?" she said.

"Just do it."

"Don't get testy," she said. "I already composed the file on Bentson. All I need is your go-ahead to send it. Reggie will be so proud."

"Since when do I conduct business to make my body-guard proud?"

"When it's the right thing to do," she said.

Damn! I'm hearing that way too often lately.

Chapter Twenty-one

Playful Cat wiped the sweat from his eyes and resettled himself in the fork of the tree. He reached up and pulled the sweatband from his head, squeezed it out, and tugged it back on. He hoped that the hunter he was watching was sweating even more. He silently willed all the biting insects in his vicinity to descend upon the other man. His right arm, crooked at the elbow, held the half-meter-long blowgun ready for instant use. He reached with his left hand, removed the visor from its pouch on his belt, and slipped it on like a pair of sunglasses. It trapped hot, humid air against his eyes, making him even more miserable. The visor was in visual amplification mode, merely bringing the image closer to his eyes like a pair of old-fashioned binoculars. He directed his gaze toward the hunter, who was perched about five meters up in a tree across the clearing. He grinned as he saw the hunter contort himself to slap his leg, detaching a fly about the size of Idaho.

Playful Cat had been taking pills to alter his body scent for the past few days. Hopefully, he smelled like a plant. Every now and then the flies managed to find him, too, and he wondered exactly how they did that. He wasn't aware of any vegetarian flies.

The clearing was small, just enough of a break in the canopy to let sunlight down to the ground. Playful Cat was close to the hunter, perhaps fifteen meters air space between them, but the hunter was watching the ground below, not the trees. His concentration was such that Playful Cat

could probably have walked right up to the base of the tree
he was in and asked him for the time of day without getting
a response.

The object of his concentration was in the clear patch
between the two of them. A goat, tethered to a stake.
Playful Cat noted with approval that a bucket of water had
been left for the goat's use. Even bait got thirsty. The goat
was cropping the undergrowth at the limit of its tether. If it
knew why it was there, it would have acted a lot more concerned. Frantic.

The International Zoo Association, IZA, of which
Playful Cat was a board member, had a repopulation program going for the Asian tiger. Nearly extinct in the wild, a
handful of the big cats lived in zoos around the world.
Sperm from a tiger in the San Diego Zoo met and fell in
love with an egg from a tiger in the London Zoo, the entire
romance initiated and consummated in a glass dish. The re-
sulting embryo was implanted in the uterus of a lioness. A
surrogate mother was used for two reasons: to spare the
precious female tiger the stress and risk of pregnancy and
giving birth, and to multiply the opportunities for successful
births. After all, once pregnant, the tigress was tied up, so
to speak.

The surrogate mother birthed her litter of one and lov-
ingly raised her false cub in an open range wildlife preserve
in Zambia. Under the watchful eyes of the rangers, she
taught her cub, so inept at first, to hunt. The half-grown
tiger was drugged, transported a continent away, and released at a site in northern India. To help the tiger adjust to
its new territory, easy kills were provided for food in the in-
terim until the tiger became the efficient solitary predator it
was meant to be. Contact with humans was minimized to
give the cat the best chance of adapting to the wild. The

program had a fair success rate and was getting better every year as the techniques evolved. It was not publicized. The low profile was to protect the animals from opportunistic hunters, one of whom was waiting uncomfortably in a tree across the clearing from Playful Cat.

Bradley Cummins was a rich old codger who had a secret room filled with trophies of his illicit hunting, the rarer the animal the better. He liked to take his women there and screw them in front of all those glass eyes. It added to his thrill, somehow. When a recently jilted lady spilled the story to a friend, it had come to Playful Cat's sensitive ears through a chain of informants. He had been watching Cummins ever since, waiting for the man's next expedition. He was surprised to find that the target of that next expedition was a product of an IZA program. He still had not discovered how the information, including the exact location of the release site, had been leaked. But he was working on it.

In the meantime, his world had narrowed to the scene in front of him. There was Cummins in a tree with a high-powered rifle, the tethered goat Cummins had set out, himself with his weapon of choice—and no tiger. Playful Cat could take the hunter out at any time, but it offended his sense of propriety to do so without a clear and urgent need. After all, maybe the rifle was for self-defense, and the man intended to whip out a camera when the tiger approached.

Uh-huh.

He removed the visor and slipped it back into its belt pouch. Sweat dripped off his nose and poured in torrents from his armpits. Floral-scented sweat, he hoped. He took a canteen from his belt and drank from it. As he capped and replaced it, he caught a movement from the corner of his eye. The big cat was directly below him. He hadn't seen the approach. He saw the cat lift its head and sniff tentatively, and he hoped that he did indeed smell like a flowering plant, or at least like something that would taste bad to one big hunk of a predator. He knew that his perch in a tree offered no protection from a determined tiger. The supple animal moved forward, padding soundlessly, a shadow among many shadows in the forest. It paused at the edge of the clearing and hunkered down, motionless except for the tip of its tail, which twitched in time with Playful Cat's heartbeat, or maybe it was the other way around. The goat had not caught the feline scent and continued to graze peacefully.

Playful Cat did not need the visor to see that Cummins had spotted the tiger. The man was positioning his rifle. No camera in evidence. Playful Cat removed one of the small, feathered darts that rode in individual pockets on a thick strap fastened to his left forearm. He inserted the feathered end of the dart into the tip of the blowgun, leaving the barb exposed. He inhaled deeply, stopping just before his maximum lung capacity. Then he raised the blowgun to his lips and finished the inhalation, sucking the dart down into the shaft toward his mouth. He had to load the dart that way, backwards. If he inserted it barb-first into the mouthpiece end of the blowgun, the poison would brush off onto the mouthpiece, and when he placed his lips against it, poison would enter his mouth.

When the feathers tickled his lips, he aimed and exhaled a hard rush of air. The dart lodged in the hunter's neck.

One, two, three.

The rifle slid from the man's hands and fell to the ground, the noise of its impact cushioned by the undergrowth, which was heavier there at the edge of the clearing than in the deep shade of the unbroken forest canopy.

Cummins remained lodged in the tree, eyes staring, a look of surprise frozen on his face.

The tiger, undisturbed, completed its stalking and pounced in a great leap on its prey. For a moment, Playful Cat thought he saw the same look of surprise in the goat's features. Then the force of the tiger's landing snapped the goat's neck, even as powerful jaws clamped down on its vulnerable throat.

Chapter Twenty-two

"Kenny, have I ever let you down before?"

"Of course not, Case. That's why I've given you such a long leash. But I've got to have something to wave in front of the boss. You understand that."

Casey sat back in her chair and sighed. She could tell by the look on his face that Kenny was not going to be cajoled so easily this time. It was time to level with him.

"Look, Kenny, I need to tell you something about this article. It's gone off on a different slant." He was silent and attentive, but a storm was developing in his normally peaceful eyes. He didn't smooth the way for her, so she swallowed and continued. "I decided it would work better as an eco-investigative piece."

Kenny reacted with an outpouring of abusive language that passed over her like a quick summer thunderstorm, lightning and thunder and tree-twisting winds. She kept her eyes fastened on his face and took it all in.

In a few minutes he ran down and just sat there, shaking his head.

"Are you telling me," he said, "that AmerNet advanced you ten thousand bucks and you have nothing—nothing— to show for it?"

"I sent you those personals on Gunner's ex-girlfriends," Casey said.

"Fluff. Goddam fluff. You know as well as I do that those are just the sidebar crap. I need something with meat on its bones. What ever happened to that personal with

Gunner? Was that imaginary too?"

"Come on, Kenny, give me a break here. No, that wasn't imaginary. The interview took place. It just went sour, that's all."

"Sour! Jesus. How sour are we talking about? You didn't get arrested, did you?"

"His bodyguard squashed the shit out of my recorder."

Kenny rolled his eyes. "So you have no quotes. How the hell are you going to write a profile with no quotes?"

"That's what I've been trying to tell you, Kenny, if you'd just listen. The piece has changed direction. I'm still working on it, it's just that it's turned into investigative work. Gunner is greed personified. I'm going to make the public sit up and take notice. By the time I finish this piece about the dam and Gunner's personal dirty dealings, they'll be crying out for blood. His."

"Is this public you're talking about AmerNet readers?"

"Probably not."

"Jesus, Case."

"I'll come through for you, Kenny. I really will."

"What have you got on these personal dirty dealings?" he said. She saw the journalist's gleam in his eyes. "Just the facts, please."

"Nothing. Yet."

"Jesus! Do I detect a personal vendetta here? Revenge for being on the squashed-to-shit side of that interview, maybe?"

Casey pressed her lips together and said nothing. He shook his head again. Twice in one conversation. No good at all.

"This is no good, kid, no good at all. There's such a thing as professionalism in this business. In the relationship between freelancer and editor. You just put that relationship in the toilet. I hope you like waiting tables, Case, or writing annual reports. Because when word gets around of an assignment botched up this bad, you're going to find it tough getting work. This thing smells of incompetence, if not outright fraud, on your part, and editors have good noses. And there's the ten thousand. AmerNet will want it back, of course."

"Word doesn't have to get around, Kenny, unless you spread it."

It was a low blow and she knew it. He had already covered for her as long as he could, far longer than she could have reasonably expected.

"I don't know what's made you like this, kid, but I'm sorry to see it. I expect that ten thousand back in AmerNet's coffers by the end of the week."

Kenny broke the connection. It was the equivalent of slamming the door in her face. She'd never seen him so riled.

Casey sat for some time at her cluttered desk. Then she rose and went to a bureau, a junky old thing that had served the needs of many in its long and undistinguished lifetime. She yanked open the bottom drawer, which caused one of the two knobs to come off in her hand. The bureau wasn't up to mistreatment. She drew out a shoebox, straightened up, and tried to shove the drawer back in with her foot. She succeeded in jamming it crookedly. The weight of the shoebox was comforting in her hands. She took it back to her desk, put it on top of the clutter, and untied the string that held the lid on top.

Inside was a layer of photos. She picked up the first one and held it up to the desk lamp. It was a young couple with eyes only for each other. The two lovers were Casey's parents, he an impoverished writer struggling to convey his vision, she a rich socialite whose presence in the photo was a slap in the face to her own parents. The smiling woman was pregnant with Casey at the time, an additional insult to her family. But they were happy, clearly thrilled to be together, even in the face of obstacles.

They had only ten years together. Her father's career was a moderate success, moderate because he didn't manage to get down in written form all the stories that consumed him, that fired everything he did with a purifying blast of passion. When he developed an inoperable brain tumor, he didn't wait for pain to incapacitate him. He hugged his wife and daughter on a Bermuda beach, left them reading under an umbrella, swam out into the ocean as far as his physical reserves could take him, and slipped beneath the waves as though he were pulling a blanket up to his chin for a cozy nap.

Casey's mother made it through two years before she joined her husband with the help of a bottle of pills. Her hold on life had been tenuous at the best of times. She was an ethereal thing, a fragile bundle of emotions and white violets anchored by her husband's devotion and by his simple daily presence. He had been measuring time and life for them both.

She wrote a letter to Casey apologizing for leaving her, for not being strong enough to wait until Casey was grown and out on her own. At the age of twelve, Casey went to live with her father's brother. Uncle Rick and Aunt Madeline were sane and warm people who welcomed her into their home and added her wholeheartedly to their own brood of four children. Nevertheless, she erected walls to keep their affection out, and her own anger and loss inside. Years later the walls were still functioning, although there were chinks and patches.

Casey traced her parents' faces in the photo with her finger, and gently touched her mother's abdomen, where baby Casey was riding inside. She put the photo aside and lifted out the rest of them, images of birthday parties, vacations, good times long gone. Stacking them out of the way on her desk, she reached inside the shoebox and pulled out a man's handkerchief. The corners had been pulled up and knotted together, making an impromptu sack that sagged heavily down toward the desk. She fiddled for a minute with the knots, unable to untie them, then used her teeth to pull. The knots came undone abruptly, and the contents spilled out over her desk, sparkling and radiant. Her mother's jewelry.

The day her mother had revealed that she was pregnant and planning to marry, she was disowned by her family. In a gesture of defiance, she stormed upstairs to her room and emptied her jewelry chest into the pockets of her trousers. She intended the jewelry to be sold to support the two of them plus the little one inside. But her husband-to-be would have none of that. They would make their own way. He tied the fabulous necklaces, pins, earrings, and bracelets in his handkerchief, and there they remained, unsold even during the tough times. Sometimes Casey's mother would get out the treasure sack and mother and daughter would play "Society," modeling the jewels and gawking at each other in the mirror, the same ornate, golden-framed mirror on the wall across the room now.

Casey picked up a diamond pendant and fastened the delicate chain around her neck. She approached the mirror to check out the effect. The diamond rested at the hollow of her throat like a glistening dewdrop, the kiss of the sun caught in its depths. She never intended to sell the jewels. They were the kind of thing that should be passed on to her own daughter, if she ever had one. But she knew that the time was right. She needed to be there, to see Gunner again. He was linked to her life somehow, like her mother was linked to that struggling author the first time she set eyes on him.

This one, she thought, taking off the necklace. I'll sell just this one. I'm sure it will bring a good price and I can pay Kenny back. I need enough for the trip to Rio, too.

Chapter Twenty-three

Rose paced around in the suite at World Power HQ. Bedroom, spa, garden dome, back again. She exercised, working her lithe body mercilessly until her leotard was soaked, then stripped and turned her face up to the cold needles of the shower, water streaming over her closed eyelids and smooth black hair. When Gunner arrived, which was not every evening—sometimes he was halfway around the world—she devoured him, climbing his body before he could get out of his suit. He joked that he was going to have to undress out in the foyer to keep down the dry cleaning bills. He could tell that she was frustrated and restless but couldn't tell why. Neither could she, until it came to her one sleepless night.

Some inner clock, keeping time with the twisted beat of her hatred, said that it was time to take action. Time to kill, time to destroy her father once again. Project Crystal was moving too slowly for the repetitive cycle of her victimization and vengeance. Like pus building inside a boil, the blackness in her could only be kept in check for a limited time. It wasn't time to kill Gunner yet, not if she wanted maximum effect.

If Gunner was off limits for the time being, there were plenty of other men in the world. Why not someone else? With that comforting thought her muscles relaxed and she slept soundly.

When she awoke in the morning, the plan was fully in her mind. It was an important day anyway; it might as well be doubly fulfilling. She sat at the computer terminal and communicated with Colleen, who was responsible for scheduling the assignments of the copter pilots. Rose asked for the use of a copter for most of the day. She wanted to go to the beach and then shopping in Pattaya, on the mainland. Colleen disapproved, since Pattaya was a town principally concerned with entertainment for males. However, there was no credible reason to deny the request, including the assignment of Mahomet as pilot, since he had promised to show Rose a new silk shop there. Rose smiled at the frostiness in Colleen's voice. She knew that Colleen had to do what the boss said, and the boss said that Rose had free run of the services. And why not? She was the future Mrs. Gunner.

Rose packed her beach bag carefully, including some clothes to toss on over her swimsuit for the trip to town. Mahomet dropped her at the fishermen's beach, and she repeated the teasing action, just as before, of bending over and giving him a good view as he left. While he was gone, she swam and visited with the fishermen.

When she got to the boat that held the man who was her connection to The Six, she received a small package from the occupant. There was a note with it from Wrongful Death. It looked like he'd done the best he could on her microbomb request. It would be undetectable up until the last fifteen seconds or so before exploding. Not as good as she'd hoped, and she'd have to take his word for it—she wasn't about to ask Reggie to check it out for her with a Tattletale. She tucked it into the waterproof bag fastened snugly at her waist. Back on the beach, muscles deliciously tired but not too tired for what lay ahead, she packed the small box into her beach bag and waited for Mahomet.

When he returned, she made quite a show of pulling on

her skirt and top over the now-dry swimsuit, letting him imagine himself pulling them off. She entered the pilot's compartment rather than the passenger's, and sat in the co-pilot's seat next to him. Her skirt was short and hugged her hips, and she made sure it rode up when she sat down. He turned a puzzled look on her that was mixed with desire. Without saying a word, she took his hand and placed it on her thigh. It rested there a moment and then began to move upward. The puzzlement vanished from his dark eyes. Lust burned there brightly.

"Take me to Pattaya," she said in her velvet voice. "I know a place there . . ."

Hours later, Rose called Colleen to complain that Mahomet had not arrived at the designated time to pick her up from town. She was stranded there and could Colleen send someone, a reliable person this time, to bring her back?

Rose slept well that night, cuddled against Gunner's side, with his arm around her protectively.

Chapter Twenty-four

Adam and Sarah Grant sipped tea on the front porch of their Appalachian farmhouse. It was early October, and the leaves were beginning to change in the wooded hills surrounding them. It was Adam's favorite time of the year. He was content to sit next to his wife and watch the wind stir the leaves. It was as if the sun's energy, kept captive all summer, escaped and glowed from the inside of each leaf. Soon wind and storms would knock the leaves to the ground, where they would rot and provide nutrients for next year's growth. There was a grand continuity to it that Adam could appreciate, a cycle that was good overall but not kind to the individual.

Sarah touched his hand. His thoughts, which had been tumbling along as lightly as the leaves swaying in the breeze, came back to the porch and the two of them sitting in the late afternoon sunshine.

"Dearest," she said, "about that new partner . . ."

It was characteristic of their relationship, that intimate way of resuming a conversation that hadn't come to a conclusion previously. It could be hours, days, or years since the last discussion, but they were always capable of picking up the threads and weaving another section of the fabric that bound them together.

"Yes. Your hunches. I'm listening." He knew from long experience that his wife was about to use him as a sounding board, but had in all likelihood already made up her mind on whatever subject she was about to raise. Usually he played devil's advocate just for the hell of it.

"I've been working with a new contact for quite some time now. It's Robert Gunner."

"Of World Power?"

"Yes. He came to me, oh, three years ago at least, with a plan to help out the Consortium for the Planet. At first I didn't take him seriously, but he was persistent. He said that the only way to have enough impact was through the megacorps. I told him that my goals and the goals of the Big Five didn't always mesh. In fact we were on opposite sides of the fence in most cases. He said that there didn't have to be a fence."

Adam snorted; he couldn't help it. "You mean," he said, "that they'll use a few token recycled products and put an aluminum can collection bin in the employee cafeteria."

"I admit that's the way it has been in the past. But Gunner was talking about a real shift in priorities, Adam."

"Wait a minute here. Have you forgotten the São Gabriel hydroelectric project? This guy's planning to flood zillions of acres of Brazilian rainforest. Not to mention all the other charming things his company does."

Sarah shook her head. "He wants me to believe that's all a sham, that he needs to maintain that image until he consolidates his position. He says that he's been purposely delaying the dam."

"What's this consolidation business?"

"Gunner has a plan to get control of the other megacorps. When he's in charge, he'll change them. Over time they'll become more and more Green. It's the start of something good, Adam. Something big."

"He could be power hungry. He'll do anything he can to string you along, then he'll drop all this sweet talk once he can jerk the strings. The only thing that's saved us this long is the fact that all the corporations are at each other's throats. Imagine the harm that could be done if they were cooperating!"

Sarah sat back in her chair. She seemed to shrink in front of his eyes, to become smaller than he'd ever seen her. Even though she was physically a small person, the strength of her character had always made her seem large.

"Don't you think I haven't thought of that?" Her voice came out as a whisper, as soft as the wind reprimanding the leaves for their prideful display of colors. There was silence between them for a while.

"Let's go back to the issue of consolidation," Adam said. "Tell me more."

She sighed. "I don't know much about it. Gunner won't be pinned down. I think I'm only seeing a little piece of the plan, but it seems to be working. At Gunner's direction, the rank and file of the Consortium acquired a large block of Superior stock, a bit here, a bit there. Somehow Gunner managed to pry most of Bentson's personal holdings away from him, so that our stock and Gunner's together make up a controlling interest. There's word that Bentson is going to retire soon. Very odd, since it seemed like he thrived on the work and wouldn't leave it until he dropped dead at his desk. Already Superior has dropped a number of projects and modified others substantially."

Adam took an ice cube in his mouth and crunched it hard. But he said nothing, so she continued.

"Another thing. Something happened between Gunner and Carlos Angeles. I wasn't involved. Angeles made a three and three-quarter million dollar personal contribution to the Consortium, out of the blue. The guy had never so much as subscribed to the newsletter before. His corporation also donated communications services for the campaign to raise money for Harmony Park in Antarctica. Previously he'd actively worked against it."

He tipped his glass back and sucked in another ice cube.

"Tamura Products is under indictment for manufacturing illegal drugs, which it was doing to prop up the sagging profits everybody's known about for months. The source of the incriminating leak hasn't been revealed, but it fits the pattern of what Gunner's been doing. Within two weeks of the indictment, Tamura Products was bought, lock, stock, and barrel, by Carlos Angeles. Tamura didn't fight it, and the purchase package was more than Angeles could possibly have pulled together by himself. He just didn't have that kind of financial backing. I can guess where it came from."

Adam shrugged his shoulders, as if to say that all this was inconclusive. Except for the purchase of the Superior stock, which Sarah had been involved in, she had nothing directly linking Gunner to these other events.

"Emil Koldabi of Frontier Enterprises died suddenly, and nobody wants to talk about what killed him. Some heavy-duty flu virus or something. He was replaced by a woman whose environmental policies are Greener than anyone—anyone except perhaps Gunner—anticipated. Marlena Rosten is taking Frontier apart piece by piece and putting it back together as a model of eco-planning, and she's cajoled most of the division heads into going along with it. In fact, I've already used some of her ideas."

Adam spit the ice cube in a marvelous arc, missing the tree he was aiming at by a substantial distance. "Shit," he commented on missing the tree. "Are you saying that you think Gunner was responsible for Koldabi's death? That there's a big conspiracy going on here and only Sarah Wilmington Grant has figured it out?"

"I don't have any evidence. Just . . ."

"Hunches."

It felt odd to talk about Koldabi's death with Sarah, even odder to consider that someone else might be out there working in parallel toward the goals of The Six, and with tactics as brutal if not actually murderous.

"So now you're telling me Gunner is a killer, that you're working with a murderer," he said. He didn't want Sarah dwelling on Koldabi's death too long. He wanted to shelter her from what he did.

"I don't know that for certain. Or maybe I do, and I've become so caught up in this that I don't care."

"Any means to an end? That doesn't sound like you, Sarah." He closed his eyes. He wondered what Sarah would think if she knew the truth about his own activities. Quite a few of his trips over the past half a dozen years were not photo assignments. In this case, the Koldabi thing appeared to have played directly into Gunner's plan.

The question remained: was that good or bad?

There was a subtle shift in Sarah's expression, something only he could have picked up.

"How about you springing for a pizza?" she said. "Cabby's has decided to deliver out this way."

"Really? We're the only customers 'out this way'."

"Well, a certain amount of influence was brought to bear. I threatened to picket them for inhumane treatment of pepperoni."

"No mushrooms," Adam said. "I hate mushrooms."

"The onions are non-negotiable."

"It's a deal." He had played the role. He had voiced her doubts for her, out loud. And she hadn't changed his mind about Gunner, but he would look into it.

Chapter Twenty-five

A few days later, Tearful Clown presided over a meeting of The Six. Only three other members were present in the conference room in the Alps. Burning Rose was on assignment, and Wrongful Death was hot on the trail of some new electronic marvel and declined to be interrupted. When he got like that, there was no use pressing the issue.

Cones of light floated down from the ceiling, illuminating the two empty places at the table as well as the four people seated there. Tearful Clown told them about Gunner and the corroborating evidence, admittedly weak, which he had been able to dig up in the intervening days since he talked with Sarah, whom he identified only as a knowledgeable informant.

"Your evidence doesn't stand well against the public record of Gunner and his company," said Chess Master. "But you believe your informant's hunch?"

"Whether I believe it or not doesn't matter," he answered. "What matters is that the informant believes it, and the informant has an excellent track record in the hunch department. We have little to lose by waiting and a great deal to lose by acting too soon."

"Then your recommendation is . . . ?"

"To suspend Project Crystal until the facts are clear."

One by one the faces around the table nodded.

"Very well," Tearful Clown said. "I'll notify Burning Rose."

Chairs scraped backward as the attendees prepared to leave.

"Playful Cat, would you stay for a moment?"

The other two left the room. He wondered for a moment what their lives were like outside this conference room. Did they have French toast for breakfast this morning in the resort's restaurant with the splendid view of the mountains, as he did? He sighed and turned back to Playful Cat, who had remained seated across the large table. They regarded each other a moment in silence.

"I think you know why I've asked to speak to you in private," Tearful Clown said. Playful Cat said nothing, just waited with the infernal patience of the hunting feline. Tearful Clown sighed again.

"I'll spell it out for you. Gunner and Burning Rose are on their way to the press conference at the dam site in the jungle. I'm not sure our agent in Rio will be able to connect with her in time. My biggest concern is that even if the message gets through, I'm not sure Burning Rose will go along with the suspension. I think there may be a personal agenda involved."

Still silence.

"I want you on the scene. Persuade her."

Black eyes glittered inside the cat mask, cold and at odds with the triangular pink nose pad. The strong jaw below the mask was impassive.

"Why me?"

"Because jungle action is your territory. Because I trust your judgment in the hot seat. And because you can be a mean son of a bitch when you set your mind to it, and that might be what's called for here."

Playful Cat's expression didn't change. They both knew what was implied. Members of The Six had never turned against each other before, but if Burning Rose didn't cooperate, she had to be stopped. The reality of it drifted over them like a foul, smothering fog. Tearful Clown wondered if he'd made the right choice. Or if the man opposite him would agree.

Maybe Cold-Blooded Serpent should go. Send a woman after a woman.

"Damn straight," Playful Cat said. "I'll be there."

Chapter Twenty-six

Cold-Blooded Serpent walked back to her room through the darkened, quiet hallways. It was almost 2 a.m. when she left the conference room. There was no exotic nightlife at the resort, unless the guests slipping barefoot from their rooms and rapping on a lover's door down the hall counted. By now the corridors were empty. The bed swapping was accomplished for the night, the vaginas lubricated, the sperm spilled. In another couple of hours, there would be activity again as wayward partners returned to their original rooms before dawn.

When the door closed behind her, she stripped quickly and tossed the iridescent outfit, patterned after a snake named Pattycake, on the floor. No longer Cold-Blooded Serpent, she was merely Katy Findlutz, rich bitch with a hobby. Several of them, actually. She walked to the large expanse of glass that dominated one wall of her room. The blinds were open. The resort complex was illuminated with lights marking the trails winding among the luxurious private cabins, as though glowing candles had been carelessly tossed down the mountainside.

It reminded her of the view from her room on Daddy's Island, with the lights of private yachts that were island-hopping in the Aegean Sea twinkling like fireflies.

To her it would always be Daddy's Island, even though it had a name and other people lived there too. Daddy came from an old Austrian family whose money had stuck to their fingers despite two worldwide wars. He had dedicated himself to increasing the family's already considerable holdings, plunging into a variety of business endeavors and investments. At forty-five, he was overtaken by long-delayed urges: he met, courted, and married in the space of a month. His bride, the guide on a museum tour he had taken, was stunningly beautiful and more than two decades younger than himself. Much more to his family's chagrin, she was Italian.

He was incapable of denying her, and when she said that she would like to have a baby right away, it didn't occur to him to mention that he didn't care much for children. If she had asked for a unicorn on a golden leash, he would have set about finding one for her.

He built a fabulous home for her on an island off the coast of Greece, visited her there often enough to be accused of neglecting his businesses, and stood by, speechless for once, as she groaned and pushed little Katherine Maria into the world. The baby wasn't even weaned from her mother's competent breasts when a boating accident with a drunken tourist turned Daddy into a single parent. Katherine Maria survived the dunking, bobbing to the surface and waving her arms gleefully at the opportunity for an unscheduled splash. Mommy always put a floatation belt around Katherine's plump tummy, but chose not to wear one on her own willowy waist, fashionably displayed in a thong swimsuit.

Daddy sank beneath the waves of his grief, and by the time he came up for air a couple of years later, Katherine's care had been given over to the Particular Parents' Total Care Company. Green uniformed nannies, with the company's initials PPTCC neatly embroidered on their collars, came and went with regularity. About every six months, the company sent a different one, presumably so that they could collect the exorbitant placement fee as often as possible. Daddy paid the bills from the household account and kept himself out of the picture, rationalizing that professionals were raising his daughter, and that he was no good with children anyway. He was never quite able to confront this miniature version of his beloved wife, complete with dancing eyes and thick black wavy hair. Instead he married and divorced a series of women, seeking in vain something that had slipped beneath the indifferent sea.

Katy grew up on Daddy's Island in the house where she was born. She was an emotional child with a hunger for affection and a hole in her heart that should have been filled by Daddy's love. She saw him infrequently, never giggled in his lap, never shared cookies and milk in the kitchen at midnight. When she was five years old, he brought her a strange present for her birthday. In a shallow bowl of slightly scummy water with an island sporting a plastic palm tree, three turtles swam and crawled. Because the present was from Daddy, she took her turtle-keeping duties very seriously. On their shells she painted in her childish scrawl the words "DADDY," "LOVES," and "KATY." She watched the turtles for hours as they moved about, spelling out DADDY LOVES KATY and KATY LOVES DADDY along with more muddled declarations. The turtles began to assume an important role in her life. She diligently learned a great deal about them, persuading her nannies to read biology books to her. When she could read, she was awestruck with the tremendous volume of information available to her by computer. She drank in the knowledge in great thirsty gulps, discovering along the way a precocious aptitude for computer applications.

It wasn't long before she discovered a certain deficiency with turtles as pets. They couldn't reflect much of the love and attention she was showering them with back onto her. It wasn't in their natures. So the next time she saw Daddy, she asked if she could have some other pets. She wasn't specific, and he didn't give the issue anything but superficial consideration (vague thoughts of ruined carpets flitted through his head) before saying yes. Katy methodically began working her way through amphibians, reptiles, and up to fuzzy puppies and kittens, studying as she went. Her acquisitions were given meticulous care by her reluctant nannies. She browbeat them into going along with her growing menagerie.

It was the snakes that sparked a special fondness in Katy. She focused her attention on one in particular, a special snake with a questing tongue and iridescent scales that flashed red or gold depending upon the angle of the light. She took to wearing it around her waist, encircling her and keeping her safe. To her it felt like Daddy's arms. Or a floatation belt.

When Katy was thirteen, she had a nanny named Hannah who was only a handful of years older than she was, more confidante than caregiver. One night as the two of them giggled in Katy's suite the conversation turned to men. Specifically, to sex.

Whether it was the wine they had swiped from the kitchen or the fact that she knew her six months' tenure would soon be up, Hannah was feeling expansive. She retrieved from her own utilitarian room a box full of books with discreet covers. The two of them curled in the middle of Katy's big bed and paged through depictions of coupling, with Hannah offering comments from her limited personal experience. Unfamiliar feelings washed over Katy like a flash flood, a burgeoning and unfocused desire. Flushed with wine, her body aglow beneath the crisp sheets, Katy allowed Hannah's warm, gentle hands to rove over her breasts, quivering stomach, and the soft mound between her legs. At Hannah's urging, she took the older girl's nipples into her mouth and sucked gently, as she would a lemon drop. The two fell asleep wrapped in each other's arms.

It was a one-time event, since Hannah was worried about getting blacklisted in the nanny business should the truth be known. But for Katy, there was a sudden awareness that there was comfort, affection, and closeness available in the world, though not from Daddy. The ticket to all those desirable emotions was sex.

She went to Hannah's room when the girl was out shopping, and studied the sex books with the same intensity she displayed when learning about her pets. When she was satisfied that she had absorbed enough, she selected a middle-aged groundskeeper as her first target. At first the man was simply bemused by her advances, then fearful of dismissal and prosecution as she persisted. He gently discouraged her, until, frustrated, she stomped away, claiming that she was going to tell Daddy that the groundskeeper had molested her. This caused the man to have a number of sleepless nights, sick with worry.

Nothing came of it for the simple reason that Katy had found another target, a more jaded and acquiescent one. In fact, she found a whole group of targets: Daddy's business associates. Periodically he entertained at the spacious home he had built for his first wife, inviting associates and spouses for a week or two. Flirting lightly, Katy would determine which of the men seemed amenable to further contact. Those she selected, she later approached brazenly, anywhere with a modicum of seclusion: an empty hallway, a little-used patio, the vine-covered gazebo. None of the men made an issue of her age, or the fact that she was the daughter of a trusted associate.

With each one, she insisted on being held in masculine arms and resting her head against a masculine chest, listening to the heart thudding inside, reverberating in her ears long after the brief moments of contact.

But it was never enough. When her heartbeat returned to normal tempo and the mingled sweat dried from her body, the need was still there. As she showered away the juices of sex, her thoughts were already on setting up the next encounter. By the time she was sixteen, she found that she had to use a moisturizer on her young skin to counter the effect of so many showers a day.

Then came the unhappiest event of her life—the loss of her mother had occurred so early that it was now an objective thing—on a day that began in ordinary fashion, with lessons from a private tutor. Katy didn't attend school; the school came to her. In fact, she did most of her work by computer, so she was able to participate in classes with a network of other young people around the world, the offspring of wealthy and reclusive parents.

In the afternoon, she went out to the gardens to do some assigned reading, taking her special pet with her. Pattycake was a Rainbow Boa from Honduras, one of Katy's first reptilian acquisitions. The Boa was amazingly responsive, and Katy had a deep and complex relationship with it that stretched the definition of love. Nearly two meters long, the snake had sloughed its skin recently and the fresh golden-brown scales underneath were splendidly iridescent. Katy unwrapped Pattycake from her waist and put the snake in the sun to doze while she did her assignment. Absorbed in her reading, Katy didn't notice when her pet slithered away on some reptilian adventure.

It was Pattycake's last adventure, for she encountered something beyond the understanding of the limited brain behind her unblinking eyes, something which did not exist as a threat when her kind evolved: a garden tractor. The blade of the mowing attachment was freshly sharpened by the diligent groundskeeper. He caught a glimpse of the snake as it disappeared, tongue cautiously evaluating this new situation, under the wheels of the tractor. By the time he stopped the machine and hopped off, Pattycake lay behind him, severed and writhing.

When Katy approached, drawn from her studies by the commotion and the small somber gathering of servants, the snake was, mercifully, already dead. She threw herself onto the grass and howled, thrusting away those who attempted to console her. The groundskeeper, the very one she had propositioned three years earlier, protested to anyone who would listen that it was an accident. Finally someone thought to bring a large box, into which the segments were loaded, removing them from Katy's sight. Abruptly Katy rose from the ground and went into the house, her mouth set in a formidable line, wiping tears away with her fists. When the family doctor arrived, he found her in her elaborate pets' quarters, quietly stroking a purring cat. He offered her something to help her sleep, which she declined in a rational voice. Since the situation seemed under control, he left her, with instructions to call if she wanted to talk about it.

The next few days passed in a haze as Katy silently relived the incident over and over, replaying Pattycake's agony, taking it into herself and letting it flourish someplace deep inside. It put out roots, took hold, and sent its tendrils throughout her, so that even the pseudo-comfort of sex failed her. It grew to be more than she could handle, so she decided that the pain would have to be shared.

She planned carefully. The drug sprayed into the groundskeeper's cabin through an air vent knocked him out in seconds. The next part was tricky. If anyone saw her, she really didn't have a believable explanation. It was dark; she simply hoped no one saw her. She levered the limp body into a cart and hooked up her two Labradors to pull it. It was a trick she had taught them when she was younger. At her urging, the dogs pulled the cart up a loading ramp and into a helicopter. It was her own copter, a present from Daddy. She released the dogs and tipped the cart up, dumping the man onto the floor. With the dogs and cart put away, she returned to the copter and positioned the body, tying the man into place on the seat she had covered with a tarp. Finally, she lifted off and set the autopilot to circle the island above the approach altitude.

When she was airborne, she gave the groundskeeper a stimulant spray to wake him up. After all, Pattycake had been awake; he needed to be awake to share the pain fully. It was a messy job, and tiring.

When it was over, she instructed the autopilot to move her out over open sea, carefully bundled the cutting tools and the pieces of the body into the tarp, and tossed them out the loading door.

The next morning, Katy let the rest of the staff know that she had dismissed the groundskeeper for negligence, and that he had already been sent away, and could someone please clean out his quarters? She examined her feelings at length and found no discord, no little voice telling her that it was wrong to do what she did.

So she did it again.

Not right away. It was several years later, after college. Daddy sent her away to college, away from the island for the first time in her life. She suspected that he had caught on to her seduction of his associates, because she was given a lecture about college being an ideal place to meet eligible men her own age, and she was told to pick an ordinary college, not something for the ultra-rich. She chose a college in Hawaii because the beach shown in the four-color brochure looked similar to the one she frequented on the island. A small touch of home.

Her roommate was a blonde named Casey, a firebrand who burned hot on one cause after another. Katy discovered that there was a lot of pain in the world to be shared, and made up her mind that she was going to be the instrument of the sharing.

Daddy was certainly right about one thing. There were a lot of eligible men.

Katy stood for a while, admiring the view of the mountainside, then went to the computer on the table by the bed. The monitor glowed to life at her touch on the keys. Keeping the visual off because of her nudity, she tapped in the number for a friend in the States. While the line buzzed, she toed her serpent costume under the bed, out of the way. Her friend's answering program intercepted the call.

"You've reached Casey Washington, you lucky devil. I can't promise I'll call back, but I will promise to consider it. Wait for the gong, then leave your name, number, and species."

"Case, this is Katydidit." She used her college nickname, which Casey had bestowed because Katy did it anywhere, anytime. "Remember a while ago you asked for shit on Gunner? Well, I've got something for you, not on him but on his new screw. Word has it that she's some kind of terrorist or assassin or something. Anyway, my source says she offed some Cabinet minister. Turned him into sidewalk stew with a microbomb. Waste of a good dick, so I hear. Suspect the lady likes sharp edges, too, as in balls applied to. Don't try any of your Little Miss Cocky Reporter with her. She's dangerous with a capital D. Stay way the hell away from her."

Cold-Blooded Serpent knew her warning would have the opposite effect. Tell Casey Washington something like that, and she'd be on it like a rattler on a mouse. Well, somebody had to do something about Burning Rose. She was sure in her heart that Rose wouldn't take kindly to anything that upset the timetable for Project Crystal.

There were soft knocks at the door, one thump, pause, two more.

"Gotta go now, Case. You take care. Gimme a call when you get in, and we'll have lunch someplace. That little place in Paris, maybe. My treat. Bye." She broke the connection, went to the door, and opened it.

Playful Cat stood there, still in costume. She reached out and tapped him on his pink nose, then drew him into the safe darkness and wrapped herself around his muscular body. He could take a lot of squeezing, as much as Pattycake could deliver. Maybe more.

Chapter Twenty-seven

Rose Shikuru sat at the hotel bar, making overlapping wet circles on the surface with her tumbler. A single thick slab of glass topped the bar, running its impressive length of perhaps twenty meters. Holographic images glowed beneath the glass. It was a beach scene complete with men and women, diminutive sun soakers a dozen centimeters high, scattered on towels in couples and alone. Jewel-like hummingbirds, the hotel's namesake, were poised in flight among the lolling sun soakers. If a person shifted viewpoint by leaning over the bar, the figures shed their swimsuits, which were scanty in the first place.

Rose was not amused.

A light, musky perfume still lingered in the air after the departure of Rose's companion at the bar. The tall woman with the cascade of red curls had slipped easily onto the stool next to Rose, and identified herself as an old friend of Ernie's. It was the code phrase Rose was expecting.

The hotel was a tourist attraction for those newly wealthy enough to still be pretentious about it. It was located in the Tijuca Forest, a one hundred-twenty-square-kilometer scrap of green, all that was left in the vicinity of Rio de Janeiro of the tropical jungle that originally surrounded the city. Hotel Beija-Flor, Hotel Hummingbird, was built into the side of a mountain, with portions of the building underneath a waterfall. It lived up to its name. The tiny birds hovered at vibrantly red blooms held up by vines that strayed across windowed areas. Their iridescent bodies were suspended between a blur of wings as they delicately supped from the flowers and then went for an after-dinner swim by darting in and out of the spray from the waterfall. Rose had already seen quite a few of the flying gems, and it was only October. In January the air would be thick with the sounds of their flights.

Rose chatted with her contact from The Six about Ernie's legendary week-long parties. For a fictional character, Ernie had quite a wild life. Then Rose exchanged addresses and phone numbers with her. Tucked inside the folded paper she handed the redhead was the latest report on a disk. After the woman left the bar, Rose discovered that the paper she had received contained a cryptic message, not the phony address and phone number she had expected. A tiny glittering teardrop affixed to the note identified the sender.

Project Crystal suspended indefinitely. Maintain current status. Do not proceed with planned action.

For a time her thoughts were ordered, running over the plan objectively, examining it for flaws. Suspended—why? Wasn't she doing a good enough job? Did Tearful Clown think that because Gunner had proposed marriage to her, that she could not carry through with her assignment? She turned her wrist so that the diamond on her finger caught the light above the bar. It flashed in wordless rebuke.

Was a replacement on the way, perhaps the willowy redhead herself, with the opulent curls and high, girlish breasts?

At some point her thoughts drifted into chaos, became a series of wordless visualizations, like a waking dream. She dipped the tip of her finger repeatedly into the circles of condensation on the bar top and transferred the cool liquid to that place between her breasts graced by the skin painting of a rose. Placed there as a symbolic reminder of her triumph over her father, it burned now as though flames licked the secret spot, and no amount of water could quench them.

An hour later, she left, leaving a generous tip and a crumpled note on the bar. Both were promptly swept away by the attentive bartender.

In the exercise niche of his suite, Gunner tried to work off the tensions of the day. He was sweating freely, and his loose-fitting shorts were plastered to his legs. For an hour he had stretched, lifted, twisted, and pushed against the patient mechanical resistance of exercise machines. Rose had come and gone. She had collected a few things from her luggage—one of them the knife she carried when she went out by herself—and then left again. She had bent over and planted a distracted kiss on his taut abdomen as he worked on a weight bench. He worried about her going out alone, but she laughed at his concern. After they were married, he was going to insist that Reggie assign her a guard. He began a flat-out run on a treadmill that surrounded him with the sights and sounds of a Rocky Mountain high country meadow on a clear July morning. Holographic bees hummed benignly, content in the flowers beside the path. A welcome breeze washed over him, carrying the mixed perfumes of wildflowers as it performed the mundane task of drying out his shorts. He slowed to a jog and then a walk, admiring the visuals. Exercise equipment certainly had its pluses. Gunner rarely got the opportunity to do in reality what he had just done electronically in a corner of his suite. These days his hunger for the outdoors was not satiated often. It came upon him at awkward times, in inconvenient places. Like now and here. Sometimes in a conference he would close his eyes and place himself on the bank of a mountain stream, drawing the blue spruce scent deeply into his nostrils, dipping his fingers into the cold snow melt tumbling down the mountainside.

That hunger for space and natural beauty occupied him more and more as he prepared to change his life by marrying Rose, and he hoped, having children with her. He and Rose had discussed that, and she had made it clear to him with a terrible wistfulness that family was important to her, too.

Gunner's father and mother were both geologists, chasing a strong interest in the transmission of earthquake forces through differing layers of rock. Chasing, yes, but in a comfortable, life-long-study way. When Gunner was young, the three of them would travel, whenever school was not in session, camping and backpacking in areas of geological interest all over the world. In fact, his first trip had been as a two-month-old infant carried in a sling across his mother's chest. Gunner always felt that the lessons he learned sleeping under the stars and hiking under the sun were the most valuable of his life.

He wanted to return to that simple way of life. He intended to move himself out of the circles of power, and center his life around home, family, and his own creative efforts. He intended a lot of things, but the drive to acquire and use power still held sway. His was a world of compromises where he struggled daily to keep his goals in sight. Periodically, they slipped over the horizon.

I'm just like that woman Casey, he thought, from the interview in Bangkok. I know what I should be doing, I just have a lot of trouble doing it.

Gunner hopped off the treadmill. He took a short, cool shower and pulled on a clean pair of shorts. He phoned

Reggie, who was in an adjacent room, and the two of them ate dinner together from room service carts. Rose was still out, occupied in some diversion that she didn't discuss with him. Reggie wanted to go over the travel arrangements for the trip to the interior of Brazil, but Gunner put him off. Miffed, Reggie grew uncommunicative, and the prospect of the pleasant after dinner rough-and-tumble conversation Gunner had been looking forward to moved out of his grasp.

It was early, only about 8 p.m., when Reggie announced that it was time for his beauty sleep. Gunner was sure that Reggie had something planned for the late evening. Whatever it was, it wasn't sleep, and it didn't include Gunner.

With Reggie gone, Gunner paced the suite and briefly considered a wild night on the town on his own. He was jealous of the casual freedom with which Rose came and went. He hoped to achieve that freedom himself, and soon, but it was not wise now. With a sigh of resignation, he seated himself at his computer to catch up on the day's events. As he did so, the phone chimed. No one had his number here except his programmed assistants, so whoever it was had already bullied his or her way through Colleen's smoke screen. He thumbed the response button, keeping visual on even though he was wearing only his shorts. He felt defiant today when it came to social customs.

Sarah Grant's image formed. He could tell that she was not her usual serene self.

"Hello, Robert. I hope I haven't disturbed you," she said. Her eyes momentarily darted about, looking at the background that his visual transmission revealed: his hotel room, with room service carts, and himself barely decent.

"No, not at all. A working evening. I just finished dinner." He waved at the room in a gesture of dismissal.

"Anything wrong? You seem upset."

At that she smiled just a bit. "I wanted to let you know that I've heard some news. About Bentson."

"What, did the dirty old man come up with some stock he's been hiding in his back pocket?"

"No. He shot himself."

"Oh."

"Apparently," Sarah continued, "he got wind of the pending charges for kidnapping and murder. He left a note for his wife asking forgiveness. He didn't specify for what."

"It's a little late for that, isn't it?" It was a pointless thing to say, Gunner knew, but the words were out of his mouth before he could squelch them. Sarah seemed genuinely concerned, so for her sake, he expressed the appropriate sentiments. "I feel sorry for his wife," he finished lamely.

"That's what I wanted to talk to you about. Would it be possible to call off Interpol now that the target of the investigation is no longer in any shape to stand trial? I've met his wife. She is a charming woman, and, I'm sure, completely unaware of her husband's doings. What purpose could it serve to make public accusations now?"

Gunner considered for a moment. There were accomplices in those murders: paid kidnappers, film makers. If the investigation were dropped now, those criminals would go free, perhaps to act again.

"I'm not sure I have much influence with Interpol, Sarah. I can't promise anything. I doubt that I can stop the investigation, but I might be able to keep Bentson's name out of it."

"Do what you can," Sarah said. "I wish you had told me what you were going to do before you took those flicks to Interpol."

"Why?" he asked. "Would you have tried to talk me out

of it? I was blackmailing him, you know. Did it matter that I cleaned him out and then betrayed him? Would you have preferred that I turned him in without wringing him out first? If I had done that, then the Consortium and I wouldn't be in control of Superior," he said. "You wouldn't have gotten your hands dirty with this. What happened to 'you're doing the right thing'?"

Sarah stood up behind her desk. She was practically shouting. "Who appointed you judge, jury, and executioner? You should have known the effect it would have on him to have this made public. He has a wife and two daughters, for Christ's sake!"

He stared at her until she broke eye contact. She plopped back down into her chair.

"I'm not cut out for this sort of thing," she said.

"And I suppose you think I am."

"I didn't mean it that way. I'm just upset. I thought I was tough but for some reason this really hit home with me."

"I'll only say this once, and then we'll drop it. Bentson pulled the trigger. You didn't. I didn't. Don't beat yourself up over it."

She sighed. "Yes, I suppose that's the attitude to take." She fixed him with a penetrating look. "Do try to spare Bentson's family."

Gunner thought of the families who were not spared, the ones whose daughters never came home. "Get some rest. You look exhausted."

She mumbled a reply and broke the connection.

While he was still at the desk, Gunner buzzed Reggie's room. It took eight rings to get him to answer, and when he did there was no visual.

"Reg, some news. Bentson shot himself."

171

"Yeah? Well, I hope the fucker was a lousy shot."

When the implication sank in, Gunner smiled. He preferred Reggie's attitude to Sarah's. Then he heard giggling in the background. Two distinct female voices.

"Good night, Reg. Sleep well."

"You too, Boss."

Gunner sat at the desk, fingers steepled in front of his face. Chalk up one more casualty, he thought. Would I do it again, knowing the outcome?

Yes, whispered the honest part of him that had received the news with minimal distress. *Yes, but I would have found a way to leave Sarah out of it.*

Gunner went through the motions of checking his mail, answering routine items, referring some to Colleen for more research. He realized he was stalling, waiting for Rose to come back. He hated to admit it, but things seemed to be shifting between them. Lately she was in a dark mood much of the time, retreating behind a private wall. During what he called her black times, she was unreachable. Some private demon gnawed at her and sometimes it seemed as if she welcomed it. Finally he flipped off the lights and lay down on the huge round bed. Rose had laughed when she saw it. He thought it was romantic in a sappy sort of way.

Later he awoke in the dark to the sound of water running. The shower was in use. He rolled over on his back and waited. He was nearly asleep again when Rose crawled onto the bed and spread her fragrant, wet hair across his stomach as she nuzzled between his legs.

Chapter Twenty-eight

Casey sank back into her seat, enjoying the music playing into her ears through tiny bud speakers. She was on a commercial flight to Rio, and the airport had been hectic. There were three seats on her side of the aisle. She was in the window seat, but no one was in the center seat next to her. The aisle seat was occupied by a Latino who had tried a conversational two-step with the attractive woman he'd had the good fortune to be seated next to, but he'd given up when her one-word responses discouraged him. She let the music work on her nerves, closing her eyes and savoring the chance to block out the rest of the world.

When she woke up an hour later, she dragged her heavy briefcase out from under the seat in front of her and opened it on her lap. Inside was a stack of folders crammed with clippings and notes. She pulled out the one with the background information on the dam project and paged through it. She dictated a few sentences into her recorder, but soon flicked it off, unable to concentrate. Images raced through her mind. Gunner's angular face by candlelight, the way his jacket skimmed his flat stomach, the crinkles next to his gray eyes when he laughed.

This guy's out of my league socially. Our one and only meeting wasn't exactly the stuff of dreams. And to top it all off, he's engaged. I know what Mama would say: Love happens. Then you have to cope, because you should never turn your back on love.

The chime that accompanied the "Fasten Seatbelt" light

brought her back to reality. The lights of Rio and the runways of Aeroporto Santos Dumont sparkled below.

She took a crowded minibus with a maniac driver who stopped at a number of hotels before he squealed the vehicle to a halt in front of her destination, the Hotel Grande, which was anything but. Certainly not the best Rio had to offer and nothing like the place in Bangkok, but at least it was paid for out of her own pocket. She lugged her case and backpack up two flights of stairs to a plain room with a tiny private bath and a phlegmatic window air conditioner.

She was going to see Gunner again, if only at a press conference. It had been right to come, even though she had to sell a piece of her mother's jewelry.

The local time of nearly 10 p.m. indicated that sleep was in order. In spite of her body telling her that it was mid-afternoon, Casey set her alarm for 7 a.m., stretched out on the thin mattress, and willed herself to sleep.

The insistent clanging of the alarm woke her. She fumbled toward it and knocked it off the nightstand, which shut it up. Discovering that she lacked a toothbrush, she ran her finger over her teeth, not succeeding in removing the scummy feel. In the lobby she found a breakfast bar, which actually was the bar, serving double duty. She helped herself to a heaping plate of cinnamon toast and a mug of herbal tea. The hot tea scoured her mouth of the previous day's airplane food.

By 9 a.m. Casey was standing outside the City Administration Building. There was a press conference scheduled. Assuming Kenny at AmerNet hadn't been a punitive bastard and withdrawn her low-level press clearance, her credentials should get her in. She handed her ID card to the guard and waited only a moment while he checked it out. She was passed through to another guard who performed a desultory search via metal detector, and then she was in the audience room.

Thanks, Kenny. That's another one I owe you.

To her surprise, Gunner was already there, seated at a table in a roped-off section of the room. On his right was the bodyguard she remembered from the Garden of the Seven Orchids Restaurant. She felt her cheeks warm as the bodyguard's eyes swept over her rapidly. He was scanning all those who entered, and he wasn't being too subtle about it. When she thought enough time had elapsed that his gaze would have moved on, she raised her head and found him looking directly at her, with recognition and what passed for a smile on his face. She hadn't taken him for the smiling sort. She watched as he tapped Gunner on the arm and gestured in her direction. Gunner looked up from the papers he had been shuffling, spotted her, and gave her a grin. He actually looked pleased to see her. She lifted her hand in a tentative wave. It was almost too much.

A fantasy flitted through her mind that he had no hard feelings from their last meeting, and had in fact been searching the world over for her.

Just then President Mengez entered, and the room quieted and got down to business. Casey took a seat on a folding chair near the back of the room. It was a very limited conference consisting of prepared statements of the mutual admiration type, followed by a few carefully screened questions, none of them asked by Casey. A photo opportunity wrapped up the session, which took fifteen minutes total. There were only five or six journalists in attendance, all of them local except Casey. The world as a whole was tired of pictures of President Mengez, who was a cheerful ham who would pose with the Pet of the Week.

After the president left the room, the rest of the journalists filed out. Gunner and his bodyguard came down the aisle, stopping at her chair.

"Good morning, Miss Washington," Gunner said. "Still working on that AmerNet piece?"

"No, I'm not. The pay was good but the cost was too high," Casey said.

"Well put. Are you planning to attend the conference out at the site?"

"I'd like to, but since I'm not exactly on assignment anymore, I don't have the clearance necessary to get in. I guess President Mengez wasn't too selective. My basic press ID got me in here." She gestured at the room, which now was emptied of its meager crew of reporters.

Gunner turned to the bodyguard. "Reggie, how about getting Miss Washington authorized for the site?"

Reggie shrugged, his face impassive. Gone was the welcoming smile, now that it seemed Gunner was letting the little mouse into the larder.

"See how easy that was? Actually, I'm surprised you didn't try to get Colleen or Fran or Sally to authorize you, given the way you got around them last time."

"I wouldn't dare," Casey said. "I think they're on to me."

Gunner reached out and patted her arm. Casey felt the gentle touch as a streak of fire that leaped through her body and lodged in her heart.

This can't be happening, she thought. Not with this man.

Casey noticed Reggie's eyes harden suddenly as he looked at something behind her. She spun around and came face to face with a gorgeous woman who could only be Gunner's bride-to-be. Face to face wasn't quite the right term; the top of the woman's head came just about to

Casey's nose. The woman's eyes, in her upturned face, bored into Casey's, then turned to Gunner. She planted a kiss lightly on his chin, then slipped her arm into his. It was an unmistakable woman-to-woman communication. *I have this man and you don't.*

Casey felt as though someone had thrown a bucket of water on her. It was more than the display of territoriality. There was something unnerving about being in this woman's presence. She remembered the look in Reggie's eyes when he spotted her and felt that she had something in common with him after all. They both mistrusted the same person.

Gunner greeted her cordially. "Hi, Sweets. Glad you could make it. If you'd gotten here a bit sooner, you could have had your picture taken with President Mengez."

Casey thought she heard tension in his voice, in spite of the warm greeting, and wondered if she was just imagining it.

"Casey, this is Rose Shikuru, the future Mrs. Gunner. Rose, this is Casey Washington, a journalist who will be covering the site ceremonies."

"Pleased to meet you, Miss Washington." Icicles tinkled in her voice. "We really must be leaving now. Are you finished here, Robert?"

"Sure. It wasn't a big production. 'Bye, Casey, see you at the site."

The three of them walked away. Casey was sure she wasn't imagining it. Gunner's words were appropriate, but his body language was saying something else.

There was trouble in paradise.

Chapter Twenty-nine

Reggie was up before dawn, out on the roof of the hotel checking and provisioning the helicopter. It was a long trip for the little workhorse, but he was somehow reluctant to hire anything larger. Gunner had taken his private jet from Bangkok to Rio. From there, the copter had carried them to the hotel in Tijuca Forest, touching down delicately on the rooftop pad like a dragonfly pausing on the edge of a lily pad. The copter had made the lengthy trip from Bangkok in the belly of a Flying Ferry, an ungainly transport plane. The pilot who accompanied the copter, a young Thai named Thanapon, groused about his accommodations on the flight. Reggie decided that the man was going to be a headache in the field. The São Gabriel project headquarters consisted of a few cabins in a clearing on the edge of the Rio Negro, a tributary of the Amazon. Only one of those cabins had air conditioning, and it sure as hell wasn't the pilot's.

The Rio Negro was over fifteen hundred kilometers of wild river. The upper stretches were not even fully explored. The dam site was located near the river's source, in northern Brazil, considerably closer to Bogotá, Caracas, or even Georgetown than to Rio. They were using Rio as a base because Gunner thought that it looked better politically. After all, the project was in Brazil. That media hoopla with President Mengez was for local consumption.

Gunner had been urged to hitch a ride to the site with a load of local dignitaries, but Reggie recommended against it. Gunner left all such matters of transportation to him.

The Boss would have made the trip by camelback if Reggie thought it advisable.

The Consortium for the Planet owned part of what they would be flying over, large tracts of jungle connected by eco-corridors fifty kilometers or so in width. The corridors permitted plants and animals in the otherwise isolated jungle areas to maintain an ecological balance. Or so the scientists hoped.

Reggie patted the copter's metal side almost affectionately, then went back to the suite's private reception area. He chatted briefly with his person on duty at the reception desk, a young woman named Ingrid. Light conversation seemed to require an effort almost beyond her grasp. He gave up and tapped the intercom.

"Rise and shine, Boss. It's time to hit the road."

When the answer came, it was in Rose's cultured voice. "Sorry, Mr. Camden, Robert can't answer right now. He's in the shower. I'll give him your message."

"Thank you, Miss," Reggie answered. He made an obscene gesture to Ingrid relating to why his boss was such a late riser this morning. Her hard face took a moment to register this intimacy from her superior, and then she let loose with an unrestrained laugh. But the moment passed quickly.

Reggie pulled on a light jacket to cover his shoulder holster. *Mustn't alarm the natives.* He buttoned the jacket partway, leaving enough open to permit quick access. He trundled down to one of the hotel restaurants tucked in a corner of the gargantuan lobby, the casual one where people like him didn't seem out of place. He ordered a dozen sweet rolls, boxed to go, and four cartons of orange juice, liter size. He charged them to Gunner's room even though he had plenty of cash on him at the moment. The habit dated from a time when Colleen, acting independently, had asked him to rein in his department's expenses. She would take note of this particular expense (Gunner, of course, would never notice), and reaffirm her opinion of Reggie as a spendthrift with the corporation's money. It pleased him to irritate her.

He never cared to examine his motives in wanting to annoy a computer program.

Back in the private reception area, he put down his burdens on the desk and dragged up a chair next to Ingrid. He tossed down several rolls and half the juice. It was a small vice of his, a blip in an otherwise exemplary diet. He loved sweet rolls and juice, any time of day, anywhere. Stolid Ingrid rejected his offer to share. Clearly she would never inflict such indignities on her body. He shrugged and downed another roll in a couple of chomps.

The door to the interior portion of the suite slid open. Rose came out first, carrying an overnight bag in one hand and a jaunty hat with a wide brim in the other. White-rimmed sunglasses lit up her face. She was dressed in tailored khaki pants and a white cotton blouse with pockets.

Reggie wondered if women ever actually carried anything in those two breast pockets.

Gunner emerged, looking refreshed, hair still damp from the shower. Reggie gave his boss an appraising look and decided that Gunner hadn't lost any sleep over Bentson's suicide. But the stress that Reggie had noted recently was still there. Gunner's default facial expression, the one he wore when not reacting to anyone or anything in particular, used to be open and relaxed. Now there were lines here, a squint there, a bit of tension written on his forehead between the eyes. Reggie ascribed it to the woman.

It was the first time he'd had a serious disagreement with

Gunner. Gunner's previous woman had decided that she was ready for marriage. Gunner wasn't. No problem. It was an amicable parting. There had been no expectation of a long-term relationship from the start, on either side. Rose turned up conveniently at the right time, when there was a vacancy in Gunner's bed. Oh, there was that story about Sun Lights, Inc. and her late father's invention. The story checked out with such literal precision that his suspicions were aroused even before he met the lady in the flesh. When he did, he formed an immediate opinion that she was not what she seemed. He couldn't pin it down, say it was this-and-that wrong. It was a whole spectrum of impressions, from the way she looked at Gunner when he wasn't aware of it to the unaccountable chill Reggie got when he made eye contact with her. Once he'd tapped her on the shoulder to deliver a message from Gunner. She turned slowly, as though she was preoccupied, her eyes seeing something not in the current reality. Cold eyes with hunger in their depths that stabbed right through him.

The kind of eyes he imagined a vampire would have.

But in this case the Boss had taken the bit in his teeth and refused to listen to Reggie. There had been a brief but potent argument. Since then, there had been no further discussion, as though Gunner was eager to brush the subject under the rug and get back to their comfortable camaraderie. Reggie went along with that. He had done what he could by making his opinions clear. After all, he didn't run the man's life.

Although Reggie treated Rose with the same degree of cool politeness from the beginning, she seemed to be very aware that he had tried to set Gunner against her. He figured he wouldn't be around long after they tied the knot. She would see to that. He might not be too far away from finding out what retirement for a cast-off bodyguard felt like.

Reggie licked the icing from his fingers and finished off the orange juice. He rose and stretched.

" 'Morning, Boss. 'Morning, Miss. Is this all the last-minute luggage?" He gestured at the overnight bag Rose carried. The rest of the luggage was already stowed on the copter.

"Yes," she answered stiffly, pressing the bag to her side.

Her action and the tone of her voice set off a tiny alarm in his head. Impulsively, he unclipped the Tattletale from his belt and moved toward her. Taken by surprise, she stepped backward.

"Just a quick check, Miss."

Rose darted her eyes at Gunner. "Is this really necessary, Robert? I thought you were in a hurry."

Her words and her quick sidling away solidified Reggie's concern. He glanced at Gunner, received an almost imperceptible nod.

"Just routine, Sweets. It will only take a moment. All the rest of the luggage was checked when housekeeping went through," Gunner said. "Who knows, maybe one of the staff has decided to blow us up."

Satisfied with the support he was given, Reggie stepped up close to Rose and flipped on the Tattletale. The first comforting beep identified his own weapon; then there was a neutral hum. He ran the device quickly up and down Rose's body—he knew he was taking liberties there, but what the hell—then held it close to the overnight bag. Instantly it beeped a warning.

Reggie moved back fast, a couple of meters, and drew his weapon from the shoulder holster. His peripheral vision registered that Ingrid had also targeted Rose, her trangun held in both hands, elbows resting almost casually on the reception desk.

A flustered Rose dropped the bag to the floor.

"It's . . . it's just my knife, my heirloom knife. Tell them, Robert," she said. Her arrogance had evaporated.

"She does have a knife, an antique from Japan that's been in her family for generations," Gunner said. His voice was neutral.

"Show me," Reggie said. "Slowly."

She knelt next to the bag and unzipped it. Reggie moved closer and stood over her, peering into the bag. He saw her questing hand brush against a small box and he tensed, ready to move if the box popped open. Her fingers pushed past it and closed on a wooden container, which she withdrew slowly. She removed the polished wood lid and held the container out to Reggie. Cradled within was an ornamental knife.

"I carry it with me," she explained, "when I go out alone, shopping or sight-seeing."

"Put it down and back away," Reggie said. Obligingly, she placed the container on the floor and moved back next to Gunner. She slipped her arm into his.

Reggie approached the knife and held the Tattletale toward it. Beep. He ran the device over the bag and even into the open top. The hum was steady. He slipped the trangun back under his jacket, switched off the Tattletale, and decided to test that line of support Gunner had tossed to him.

"I'll keep this knife safe for you," he said as he scooped up the wooden box. "You won't be doing much shopping where we're headed, alone or otherwise."

Gunner hesitated a fraction of a second, then chimed in. "Rose, I think that would be for the best. Reggie will take good care of it. It looks like it should be in a museum, anyway, not carried around where it could be lost." He kissed her forehead. "Besides, when we get back from São Gabriel, I'm going to ask Reggie to assign you a bodyguard. The future Mrs. Gunner shouldn't have to worry about carrying knives."

Reggie nodded in the direction of Ingrid, whose weapon had disappeared beneath the desktop. "Ingrid would be perfect for the job. I'll see to it when we get back to Bangkok."

Rose didn't even spare Ingrid a glance. Her eyes were focused on Gunner's face. "Thank you, Darling. You're too good to me." She gave Gunner's hand a squeeze. Reggie noticed the dual spots of color that smudged her pale cheeks and wondered what kind of emotions were roiling around inside her.

She zipped the bag and swept it up onto her shoulder.

"Rose, could you put on your business hat for a moment?"

Gunner was seated at his desk, head bent over a written report as the helicopter resolutely covered the miles. His comment roused Rose from near-sleep. She had been relaxing on the couch, thumbing through a magazine.

"Mmm?" she mumbled.

"Oh, I'm sorry. I didn't realize you were napping. It can wait. Go back to sleep."

"It's okay, I'm awake now." For emphasis she used the thumb and forefinger of each hand to prop her eyes open wide. It gave her a comical expression. Sometimes when she was unguarded, she seemed so vulnerable, just the nervous young woman who had entered Gunner's office with a briefcase containing all that was left of her father's work.

It was that woman, Gunner thought, that he loved.

Other times she was a stranger, a woman with edges so sharp they could draw blood at a touch. It was glimpses of the vulnerable Rose that kept him going, those flashes of pure light behind the storm clouds.

Since that evening in the Hotel Beija-Flor, when Rose had reported she'd met an old friend in the bar, there had been mostly storm clouds from her, with precious few flashes of light. Something was troubling her, but his gentle efforts to get her to talk about it had ended in frustration.

"I just thought you'd like an update on Sun Lights."

"The last I heard," she said, "there were major production problems. Too bad. Father would have been pleased to see something come of his invention."

"Stability's the major concern. The globes react with common substances, like water, and turn into little piles of dust. Not cost-efficient, since manufacturing costs required that they stay functional for at least a couple of years."

"It's a wonder the samples I had lasted so long."

"Yes, I wondered about that. Nothing we came up with lasted more than a few days. But I guess you were careful with them because they were all that you had left of your father's work." Gunner stood up and walked over to the couch. He seated himself next to Rose and took both her hands in his.

"What I wanted to tell you is that the research team has been improving the stability. They found out that the fewer contaminants there were in the crystalline structure, the greater the stability. So the plan is to manufacture them in space, where crystalline structures can be formed almost without impurities. The prototypes done in the simulator look good. Very good. This may be it, Rose, a clean energy source to bridge the gap until fusion becomes practical. Your father will get the credit. And so will you, for bringing his work to the world's attention."

As Gunner explained, he noticed that the expression on Rose's face changed, from regret at the initial problems to consternation when he told her of the potential solution. It was not the reaction he expected. Puzzled, he took her chin in his hand and turned her eyes up to meet his.

"Is there a problem? I thought you'd be happy."

"It's nothing," she said. "I have a headache. I think I'll go back to my nap now." She pulled away from him and arranged herself on the couch with her back to him.

Gunner was confused and disturbed. He had known all along that this woman had facets that were hidden. He had hoped that his love would draw out the hurt coiled inside her. Not for the first time, he allowed himself to think that the hurt might be too deep for his love to soothe.

Rose's right hand, which was chest-high in front of her body, away from Gunner's view, clenched tightly, fingernails digging into her palm. Things were not going well at all. First Project Crystal was put on hold. Then her knife was taken away. Now Gunner might find a way around the flaw in Chess Master's invention. It was never her intention to give him something that actually worked. After a few moments she brought her palm to her mouth and silently licked away the little ribbons of blood that had formed. She didn't want them to fall on her spotless white blouse.

Chapter Thirty

Mr. Shikuru was a successful man by most standards. He had a lovely wife, an intelligent and precocious daughter named Yachi, and a good business. He owned a fish processing plant where local people brought their daily catch. The business had been started by his great-grandfather. He was the wealthiest man in the small Japanese village where he, and his fathers before him for generations, had grown up. In fact, his business acumen had attracted national attention, and the future looked bright. He was the one the villagers turned to for solutions to their problems, large and small.

But that was not the whole story.

Viewed from within his family, Father was a horribly cruel and disturbed man. The earliest awareness little Yachi had was of lying in a swinging cradle at the age of two. While Mother sat crying, Father swung the cradle higher and higher while Yachi held onto the sides, terrified of falling out. His face loomed over her, laughing, drowning out Mother's soft sobs. Finally, he grabbed the cradle, stopping it abruptly at the highest point. She tumbled out, landing hard on her knees. He scooped her up and put her back into the cradle, beginning the cycle over again.

There were many variations of this activity, all of them involving helplessness, terror, and pain on her part.

As Father's business grew, he began to travel, and was away from the house for long stretches of time. Things were better then, but always he came back, and the terror came back with him. Mother was not immune. He punished her physically and emotionally for not having a son, for imagined infidelities, for serving his tea too cool or too hot. Yachi squeezed back her tears so many times that eventually she couldn't cry at all. She hated and resented Mother, because Mother was so helpless. She raged inside when Father grabbed Mother roughly and tore her dress, fondling Mother's breasts without caring that she, Yachi, was present. She ran from the room, unable to face her mother's frightened eyes, deserting her to the brutal attentions of her husband.

The horror escalated when she was thirteen. Father was convinced that Mother was fornicating with every man in the village, right in his own bed. He was obsessed with her impurity, told her that her footsteps sullied the home, told her that there was no whore like her in all history. There was no basis for his claims, not even the slightest suggestion of impropriety.

Then came the day, the black day.

Yachi and her mother were working outdoors, gathering herbs for cooking. Mother was drilling Yachi on her lessons as they worked. Father was abroad, or so they thought. A delivery man came to the house from a florist shop in a city far away. It was quite an event. A beautiful vase of roses was unloaded from the van, followed by a box gaily wrapped and tied with red ribbons. Mother took the roses inside and fussed over them. She read the card: *Roses are for love.*

Then she lifted the box from counter to table. As she did so, she noticed that one corner of the box was soggy. Her fingers nearly went through the cardboard. On the counter was a red smear. A terrible look crossed her face, then a hard mask closed over it, the mask she wore when dealing with Father. She sent Yachi from the room with a word and a look. The girl did not go far. She went outside to a low kitchen window and peered in. Mother removed the ribbons slowly and took the lid off the box. She gasped in horror and stepped back suddenly, knocking both box and vase off the table. The vase shattered, scattering roses on the floor. Among the flowers was a severed head, bloody, face contorted in a final grimace.

The daughter fastened her gaze on the head, wanting to look away, but unable to do so. It was the gardener, a young man who had shown kindness and a smile to her and her mother. Father stepped into the kitchen. He wasn't traveling at all. He had been hiding somewhere, watching the whole thing, watching Mother's reaction. He told Mother that only half the job was done. He had taken care of her lover, but she must cleanse herself. He disappeared into another room.

Yachi was paralyzed. Why couldn't she shout or run for help? Why couldn't she do anything? Mother collapsed to her knees. When Father returned he was carrying a small wooden box and the sword that had always hung on the wall as part of a display.

No! No!

Father told Mother again that she must cleanse herself, finally and forever. She shook her head no. Father said that if she didn't have the strength to do it herself, he would do it for her, and then would purify Yachi as well.

At the mention of her own name, the girl nearly swooned, but still she did not run for help. She was frozen in place, clutching the window frame with her thin fingers. Mother took the box, tears streaming down her face, and removed the small knife within. She ran her finger over the edge of the knife, bringing a thin red line welling up. Father

189

urged her to be strong. Her shoulders shook as she grasped the knife with both hands and turned the blade toward herself.

No! No!

The knife flew toward her abdomen. Mother slumped suddenly but did not topple from her knees. Instead, she raised her head and locked eyes with her husband, defiant in the final moments of her life as she had never been during the long years of it. She drew the knife across her body. Blood spilled, so much blood. She dropped the knife and clutched the gaping wound. Pain distorted her features, but she uttered no cry. An endless interval went by, measured in spouts of blood from her still-beating heart. Outside the window, Yachi was numb.

It isn't real, she told herself. It's a nightmare.

At last Father nodded, a grudging nod won at a terrible price. His sword whirled, faster than Yachi's eyes could follow, and Mother's headless body tumbled forward. The head rolled through the scattered roses to lie next to the gardener's.

Yachi knew, beyond a doubt, that her mother had made an honorable end in Father's view, and that her own life would be spared. Her mother's agony had bought life for Yachi. Enough cleansing had occurred to still the beast that dwelled in Father's mind. For the moment, at least.

She turned and was violently sick. The motion at the window caught Father's eye. He leaned the sword against the table, bent over, and picked up a rose from the floor. He went outside and found the girl slumped over under the window. He drew her to her feet, muttering all the while.

"There, there, little one. It's over now," he said. He held out the flower to her. There was a drop of her mother's blood gleaming on a petal.

"Roses are for love," he said. Father tucked the flower into her hair above her ear. His hand traveled down her cheek and continued moving down. He opened the top of her blouse, exposing her budding breasts to the warm sunshine. His hand trailed across them.

"You're so perfect . . . so young and pure."

Yachi began humming to herself, a gentle tune her mother had used to soothe her. Father fumbled with the fastenings of her skirt with one hand while reaching for the front of his trousers with the other.

"You're safe now," he said. "No other man will have you."

On her twenty-first birthday, Yachi changed her name to Rose, and had her namesake painted between her breasts. The next day she killed Father with the same knife Mother had used on herself. Except that Rose didn't bother to bring along the sword for the stroke of mercy.

Chapter Thirty-one

Wind-in-the-Branches squatted at the edge of the stream, his head at the level of the lush growth of ferns. His body was bare except for the briefest of coverings wound around his hips and between his legs. He spoke a brief prayer of thanks to the God of Flowing Waters for the gift he was about to accept. He cupped his small brown hands, dipped them into the cool water, and drank thirstily.

His pack, which was woven of bark flayed into flexible strips, was nearly full. Many small animals had heard his hunter's plea and come forward to offer themselves as sustenance to him, his mate Sunshine-Above-Trees, and the small unnamed one she carried within her belly. Still squatting, he opened the top of his pack and removed a slender stone bound to a piece of wood, smoothed by the handling of many of his fathers. It had passed to him when his private hair grew as thick as the leaves above his head. The cutting edge of the stone was freshly worked. It would slice cleanly.

He closed his eyes and listened to the sounds of the world all around him, the familiar barks, whistles, and trills that were always there, night and day, the background music of his life. His mind floated with their lilting melody for a moment, and he let himself be clasped in the gentle embrace of the Goddess of Waking Dreams. Drops of water, which pattered on the broad leaves far above his head, ran down a leaf, a branch, a flower, until they plopped softly on his unresisting head and shoulders.

Tilting his head, he accepted drops on his tongue. They tasted of the golden powder that dusted the inner mysteries of flowers. He breathed deeply, sucking in the smells, because to smell a thing was to make it part of you forever.

Once, in his wanderings, Wind-in-the-Branches had come to the edge of the world. It was a place where there were no leaves above and ferns below, only bright sky and bare dirt. He had held his breath as he ran away, until it became a great pain in his chest, so as not to take in the smell and make that strange place part of him.

He began to croon softly, a rhythmic sound like the flowing of water over stones. Soon he was rocking back and forth on his ankles. Eyes still closed, he suddenly plunged his left hand into the shallow water and drew forth a wriggling fish as long as his forearm. With his right hand he brought the stone knife down in a powerful arc, severing the head. He thanked the spirit of the fish, which had now fled its body, for the gift of sustenance.

Expertly he cleaned the fish, reverently placing the innards back into the stream, and filleting the beautiful pale flesh. From his pack he removed a small pouch and scooped a small quantity of red paste into his palm. He rubbed both hands together to distribute the paste evenly and then rubbed each piece of fish, giving it a light coating. It would keep the fish from spoiling until he got home, where it would be preserved by air-drying for several days over a framework of sticks. No time for that now. He wrapped the fish in damp leaves plucked from a nearby shrub and tucked it all into his pack, including the knife, which rested on top. With a satisfied hum, he hefted the pack and continued on his way. His hunting trip was over.

He would be sharing pleasure with Sunshine-Above-Trees before the world darkened twice more.

Chapter Thirty-two

The Rio airport at dawn was like any other airport at that time of day: few passengers and a lot of crates.

Casey lowered her rump on an item of cargo, one of a seemingly endless number of shipping crates piled at the gate. She noticed that the crate bore the StyroCycle brand. StyroCycle was brand new on the market, the brainchild of Tamura Products. It was a material obtained by mining Styrofoam cups and fast-food containers from landfills. She remembered reading a pirated internal memo from Tamura a couple of years ago that described StyroCycle as marginally profitable and recommended suppressing the development. Evidently there'd been a change of heart. StyroCycle products were just beginning to appear on the market.

Ticket in hand, Casey waited for her flight to be announced. She was taking a cargo jet from Rio to the river town of Manaus. It was a four-hour flight, unless the pilot decided to make some unscheduled stops. She had hired a private helicopter to take her from Manaus to the dam construction site.

She figured she had at least an hour before departure time, so she stood up, stretched, and went in search of a phone. She found one in a corner that didn't smell too badly and inserted her GlobeCom card. Nothing happened. She gave the phone a whack with the palm of her hand and it whirred to life. She tapped in the number for her Maui apartment, then the codes to play back her messages.

In the darkened space of her apartment, her answering

machine responded and displayed a directory of half a dozen messages that were new. Three were from Kenny. She wasn't ready to deal with those yet, so she marked them "hold." She prioritized the remaining three, putting an intriguing anonymous one first and letting the other two default by date.

The first call turned out to be a come-on from a man she had met at a seminar on homeopathic medicine. He must have been more impressed with her than she had been with him. She pressed the pending key, which would indicate to him that his message had been received and read, but that there was no response yet. Casey rarely used that feature. It irritated her when someone else pended her, but she figured (with selective memory operating blatantly) that anyone who deliberately erased his ID from a message deserved to be pended. The second message was from a man named Allen Greatwing, an influential friend whom she had contacted for information about Gunner or World Power for her research. She read the message eagerly, but it contained only an invitation to join some friends vacationing in Italy. Disappointed, Casey responded that a vacation was out of the question due to work pressures and thanked him for the invitation. As she was about to press the send key, a small hand brushed her arm.

"Hey, lady!"

Casey turned and saw a boy no more than six or seven years old.

"Come now, lady, or plane take off without you!"

Casey glanced over her shoulder at a clock on the wall. It was still forty-five minutes before the scheduled departure. There had been no announcement of boarding.

"It's not time yet," she said to the boy, who was now tugging at her elbow.

"Plane go when pilot ready. Pilot ready now. I see this, come get nice lady," the boy said. He looked up at her face with mute appeal.

Casey sighed. She turned back to the phone, quickly sent the message to Allen Greatwing, and cut the connection. She hadn't been able to get to the third message, the one from Katydidit. She was curious what her old friend had to say, but catching that plane was top priority.

"Thank you," she said, digging into her waist pack for a coin. She patted the boy's shoulder and was rewarded with a stunning smile.

This kid will go far.

She hurried back to the gate and discovered that her coin was well spent. Another couple of minutes and the flight to Manaus would have left, stranding her in the airport until tomorrow.

Gunner's copter settled in an open spot, away from the cabins that had sprung up in the clear-cut area of the forest like unnatural mushrooms. Reggie saw to the unloading of luggage and supplies while Gunner remained inside, working at his desk. Rose whisked herself away to the VIP cabin, brushing by both of the men like a blast of Arctic air.

The cooling system in the resting copter was barely keeping the tropical heat at bay, and Gunner was sweating a little. In the privacy of the office, he slipped out of his pants and shirt and lounged about in his shorts. He was trying out the wording of his opening speech for tomorrow's press conference on his three computerized assistants. Although he knew they were each handling streams of additional activity, it appeared to him as if he had their undivided attention. The three were trading jibes mercilessly, enjoying themselves, mostly at his expense. He entered into the thick of it good-naturedly, and somehow the speech took shape in record time. It was productive working with them in this mode, not to mention fun. He printed a copy of the final version to take with him tomorrow, although he rarely needed to consult notes when speaking in public.

It was one hell of a speech. Gunner was planning to reveal that the five megacorps were about to form an international organization called the Borrowed Earth Coalition. The name came from a Native American saying: We have not inherited the earth from our fathers, we are borrowing it from our children.

The coalition was still a fragile one, hammered out with behind-the-scenes maneuvering, the sheer force of Gunner's personality driving the process. The pragmatist in Gunner knew that it would take time for the effects of the coalition to be felt, but the idealist yearned for instant results. In one area, at least, the results would be instantaneous. He would be able to give up the pretense of the São Gabriel project. It had been painful to be thought of as an exploiter.

There was something else, something that Gunner hesitated to acknowledge even to himself. He liked the power of being who he was, where he was, that heady feeling of making the world's businesses and governments dance to his tune. It would be hard to step down when the time came.

He had been counting on the promise of his life with Rose to ease the way. Now that prospect, so bright just a couple of months ago, was beginning to fade, as Rose's black moods threatened his own equilibrium. He could foresee a time when he might have to distance himself. Try as he might to accept Rose as her own person, he couldn't help making comparisons between her and Liza, his first wife. He had lost a lover, a companion, and a friend when Liza died. With Rose, he had come to believe, he had found only a lover, and perhaps a manipulative one at that. For a time that had been enough. Would it be enough for the rest of his life?

But he was still caught in her web of sensuality. The sudden intrusive memory of her pressing the curves of her dancer's body against him, the sweet hollow at the base of her spine, the saucy tilt of her hips as he entered her, stabbed at him so powerfully that his erection strained against his damp cotton shorts.

Chapter Thirty-three

Even in ordinary clothing, Playful Cat was an impressive sight. When he was decked out in the form-fitting costume he wore at meetings of The Six, he looked like some kind of superhero from a movie, but even without it there was no mistaking his powerful presence. He moved restlessly from one rail to the other on the deck of the tourist boat chugging its way upriver, laboring against the stubborn current of the Rio Negro.

When he got to the airport at Manaus, he made an annoying discovery. There were no private helicopters available to take him to the site of the press conference. None. Journalists had already hired the few that served the area. Furious inside and out, Playful Cat bowed to the facts and hired a boat and its crew of two men. The boat was designed to take tourists on short jaunts down river and back, perhaps half-day trips. Now it was laboring against a river that, while still navigable at this point, did not seem inclined to make the passage easy.

He had started out one step behind the target and had never caught up.

Playful Cat had calmed down enough now to be philosophical about how a man can be tripped up by the small things, the things he takes for granted. It was a humbling experience. Sweating, he shaded his eyes and looked upriver.

Chapter Thirty-four

When Gunner awoke the next morning, Rose was propped up on a pillow watching him. He reached lazily for her, but once she saw that he was awake, she threw the covers back and hustled him out of bed. She ran her hand across his abdomen and then moved it lower, until she touched his pubic hair, which was gummy with their secretions of the night before.

"This boy needs a good cleanup. Come with me," she said, taking his hand. There was a shower stall with a curtain built into the corner of the cabin. She turned on the water and adjusted the temperature to slightly less than boiling. Then she pushed him in, and stepped in after him.

"Ouch!" he complained. "Are you trying to cook me for breakfast?"

"Nonsense," she said, maneuvering the washcloth into an interesting spot, "a little heat will just open your pores."

"When I want my pores opened, you'll be the first to know." He reached behind her slippery body and nudged the cold water control. "Ah. Much better."

"Barbarian. The primary benefit of civilization is a truly hot shower."

Gunner was delighted with her light mood. It was as though whatever had been weighing so heavily on her mind had disappeared like a night fog burned away by the sunrise.

"So let's be uncivilized," he said. "C'mere, wench." He kissed her until they both came up sputtering under the flow of water. A moment later the fickle plumbing needled them with ice cold water, driving them screeching from the shower stall. Gunner reached back in and twisted the controls, shutting off the water. He and Rose collapsed on the bed, laughing and rubbing each other playfully with towels. Gradually the towels were forgotten.

Later, while Gunner was shaving, Rose laid out his clothes for the press conference. Rose was wearing one of his shirts, with the sleeves rolled up so she could move her arms freely. She kept up a light banter with Gunner. Her reflection in the mirror showed him that she was rummaging in her tote bag, and a chill went through him.

Had Reggie given her back the knife?

Then he tossed that thought away. *And what if he had? Christ, I'm getting ready to marry this woman. I can't be thinking things like that.*

He was relieved as he saw her draw out the small velvet box and place it on the nightstand.

Gunner moved behind her, and she rested easily against him, his arms about her waist.

"It's been a good morning," he said softly into her neck. He began to unbutton the shirt she was wearing, and he was growing hard against her buttocks. She swayed against him, humming that familiar tune of hers, her fingers stroking the skin painting between her breasts. Then she pulled away.

"It's time for you to get ready," she said. "It's only forty-five minutes until the press conference."

"Aren't you the clock-watcher this morning," Gunner said. "I only have to walk from one end of the clearing to the other to get there."

She scowled at him with an exaggerated sour look on her face. He stuck his tongue out at her.

"I guess it wouldn't hurt to get there early," he said.

201

"Reggie may hate spontaneous photo opportunities, but the press loves them."

Gunner hated to spoil the mood, but he put on the business clothes she had arranged on the bed. She dressed in a practical outfit of sturdy cotton pants and blouse.

"I thought you were coming with me. Isn't that outfit a little plain for the eyes of the world?" Gunner asked.

Rose averted her eyes for a moment. "To tell the truth, I'm a little tired. I was too excited to get a good night's sleep last night. Besides, I want the eyes of the world focused only on you. It's your day to shine."

"Okay, Sweets, but you're not getting out of the reception tonight back in Rio that easily. I've been known to sweep a lady off her feet on the dance floor."

"Just you make sure it's this lady," Rose said, making her lips into a perfect red pout. "Besides, I'll be better by then. I can nap on the copter."

He kissed her lightly on the cheek and turned to go.

"Don't go yet. I have something for you." He waited, and she came forward with the velvet box. "Open it," she said.

Inside was a beautiful red silk rose, an intricate bud with a single green leaf. She tucked it into his lapel.

"I made it myself."

Chapter Thirty-five

Casey leaned against the wall of one of the cabins. Sweat had soaked through her blouse in places, forming little crescent moons under her breasts and a damp patch on her back. She was next in line to use the only public phone at the site. Her cell phone didn't have global access, and she was definitely out of her home territory, so she resigned herself to waiting. The area was swarming with journalists, every one of whom had a nervous editor who didn't like to be out of touch. She thought of Kenny and smiled. She hoped that she would be able to patch things up with her old friend eventually, but she knew that she had cut deeply into his trust. It would be a long process to rebuild it.

Just then there was a minor commotion at Gunner's quarters. Reggie, who had been lounging against the door sparring verbally with the journalists, straightened up as the door opened. Gunner walked out. Casey looked at the phone, sighed, picked up her camera, and stepped out of her place in line. The messages—the three from Kenny that might present a chance to apologize, and the one from Katydidit—would have to wait, again. By the time Casey approached the crowd, Gunner was making his way across the clearing toward a rudimentary stage and podium. He stopped frequently to chat with the reporters and pose for pictures. At this rate, he was just barely going to make it to the podium in time for the live broadcast.

She elbowed her way in until she got a close look at the man she had met for lunch and followed around the world.

Casey turned and looked back at the cabin from which Gunner had emerged and saw Rose, her exquisitely lovely face framed by the crude window. Rose's eyes were fastened on Gunner, and she followed his every move intently until the crowd hid him from her view.

The group moved along in amoeba-like fashion, flowing around obstacles like the copter, which was parked on a pad near the end of the clearing. A man made his way through the crowd, carrying a little girl on his shoulders. He tried to approach Gunner closely, but was stiff-armed away by Reggie. Casey was just near enough to hear the exchange. The man, a supervisor in the construction crew, explained that it was his daughter's birthday, and that she would like to have her picture taken with Gunner.

Gunner, having heard, nodded to Reggie and took the little black-haired girl in his arms. As he held her, she smiled from ear to ear at the cameras. Casey and a dozen others with cameras pressed the shutter releases just as the girl planted a big smack of a kiss on Gunner's cheek. When he set her down, he knelt next to her for a moment and whispered in her ear. Then he took the silk rose from his lapel and put it in her hair, as an impromptu birthday present.

As Gunner moved on toward the platform, the girl and her father were left at the fringes of the crowd, then they were out of the group entirely. A couple of journalists stayed behind, questioning the little girl, who beamed and fingered her present.

Gunner reached the platform, stepped up, and stood behind the podium. The crowd began to quiet for the speech. As the level of noise dropped, Casey heard a beeping noise with an urgent tone to it. She'd heard it once before, when an activist tried to smuggle a bomb into a press conference she was attending. It was the sound that security personnel hope they never hear—a Tattletale warning of an imminent explosion.

Usually it was the last sound they heard.

As Casey stood frozen, Reggie shoved Gunner down behind the heavy podium and shielded him with his own body. His eyes scanned the crowd as he shouted a warning.

"Everybody down! There's a bomb!"

His words freed her from stasis. Casey threw herself down on the ground at the base of the platform. She focused on Reggie's face and followed his gaze.

From his position on the raised platform, Reggie was looking at the little girl standing some distance away. She and her father had not reacted to the warning and were looking puzzled.

His eyes locked onto the silk flower Gunner had given the girl. Casey watched indecision play over his face. She could tell that he did not want to leave Gunner. He drew the trangun from beneath his shirt and thrust it into Gunner's hand. Then he erupted into action, launching himself off the platform. He rushed toward the girl at full speed, arms pumping.

Others were shouting, but the noise seemed distant. Flattened to the ground, her own heartbeat thundering in her ears, she watched Reggie race toward the child.

And not make it.

A burst of brilliance, a blinding yellow and orange fireball, assaulted Casey's eyes. She squeezed them shut and pressed her face into the yielding ground. The noise and blast force of the explosion rolled over her.

In the silence that followed the explosion, she twisted onto her side, dazed, and propped herself up against the edge of the platform. Blood oozed from a gash below her knee, but she couldn't feel it. Pain was just out of reach, waylaid by the temporary logjam of signals into her brain. Seconds later, she became aware of two things simultaneously. Her right leg hurt like hell, and someone was shouting.

She pushed up straighter and swiveled her head, which she immediately regretted. Her vision seemed to move more slowly than her head, like a motion-dampened camera that lagged behind when panned. As her vision cleared, she spotted Gunner just beginning to stand up. The heavy podium had toppled over on him, and he had pushed it away.

A thrill went through her. He was all right!

She turned her attention to the crowd. All around her, people were beginning to move. Some were lying on the ground moaning. Others were lying still. She averted her eyes from the blast site, even though there was nothing to be seen on that spot except scorched earth. Reggie had either been blown to bits or thrown backward by the force of the blast. If he had been thrown backward, then he was one of several crumpled forms nearby. No one approached her. The others were still recovering. There would be no help from any of them right away. She was on her own.

From the corner of her eye, Casey caught a glimpse of someone moving near the cabins. It was Rose, and she was lifting something in front of her with one hand—a weapon! She was aiming at Gunner!

Casey tried to shout a warning, but it came out a mumble. She pulled her body upward and threw herself clumsily at Gunner, knocking him off his feet just as he was rising unsteadily. Something sizzled in the air next to her head, then again below her waist. Her injured leg buckled beneath her. She tasted bile in her throat as she struggled to keep control of her body. Casey reached out and grasped

Gunner by the shoulder, then cried out when her fingers sank into a pulpy hole rather than resting on his firm flesh.

Oblivious to the danger of more gunfire and the stabs of pain from her leg, she put her hands in Gunner's armpits and dragged him backward until they were both behind the scant protection of the fallen podium. He was conscious and tried to raise himself, but she pressed him down.

"Don't move," she whispered. "Rose is trying to kill you. We have to get to a safer place."

He nodded. "Reggie?"

"Don't know."

Casey could see his eyes harden as he clamped down on the pain. She looked around for shelter. The helicopter was the closest thing that was enclosed. She licked her lips.

"Can you walk?" she said. "We have to move away from here." Again, he nodded.

"Wait," he said. He reached his good arm out from behind the podium and grabbed the trangun Reggie had given him. He had dropped it when Casey knocked him aside. Twisting, he tucked it into his belt.

"I'll go first," she said. "When I get to the copter, come after me."

The fact that he didn't protest worried Casey. He might have injuries other than the wound on his shoulder. Casey crawled out from behind the podium. She could see activity, but still no one came to help. She spared a glance over her shoulder at the cabin where she had last seen Rose, but the woman was nowhere in sight.

She could be anywhere by now, including inside that copter.

After crawling a few meters, she pushed herself up and stumbled along upright, limping heavily. She was unable to move fast, but there was no attack. She didn't know what to make of that, but accepted it gratefully. By the time she reached the copter, she dared to hope that something had happened to Rose, that someone had stopped her or at least distracted her. She yanked open the passenger door—what if it had been locked?—and pulled herself in. She was relieved to see that Gunner was behind her, crossing the open space in a zigzag path. Just as he got to the pilot's side, a bullet zipped past the windshield and struck the copter centimeters from his head.

He pulled himself up into the seat with his good arm, then slammed his palm on the starter button. As the machine responded, he yanked the controls. The copter jerked and lurched into the air like a lumbering insect. Another bullet hit on Casey's side and sliced through the door, missing her narrowly and burying itself in the control panel. Then the copter collected itself and shot forward in a steep ascent.

Chapter Thirty-six

Rose watched from the window as Gunner walked through the crowd of journalists on his way to make a speech. She knew that the speech was very important to Gunner, but she couldn't put her finger on exactly why. No matter. Whatever it was, soon it would be eclipsed by her triumph.

Destroying the despoiler. She savored the thought. The other times, with other men, she had gotten a glimpse of this feeling, this ultimate power, this lack of helplessness. But never so strongly as this. It was a euphoric feeling, as though the power formed a bridge across the chasm of despair in her soul.

Her family would applaud her success. She thought of them fondly—Tearful Clown, Chess Master, Cold-Blooded Serpent, Playful Cat, even Wrongful Death with his brittle voice and brittle heart. Their approval would strengthen the bridge, reinforce the power. She was so glad she had found her family after all these years—the black years. Maybe now little Yachi Shikuru could stop hurting inside.

She stroked her fingertips over the painted rose between her breasts. The skin felt hot, a little patch of warmth that betrayed the fire burning out of control beneath.

Gunner wove in and out of her view. She noticed a man working his way inward through the cloud of journalists that surrounded Gunner like so many gnats. He was carrying a girl on his shoulders, a smiling girl with straight black hair like she had, happy to be here today, riding on her father's shoulders above the crowd. Rose remembered a time when Father had carried her on his shoulders through the streets of the village. All the village girls had looked at her with envy, up there atop her rich father. She would have given anything to be one of them instead.

By the time Rose returned from her memories, the little girl was no longer perched above the group. Anxiously she scanned for the child.

There she is, on the edge over there . . . What's that red on her shoulder that wasn't there before? Oh, no, she's holding the rose! Should I try to save her?

Rose gripped the edge of the window frame hard enough to dig her nails into the soft wood. *No one saved me . . .*

Then her thoughts twisted in another direction, and the girl was forgotten. *How dare he give away my present? I made that rose with my own two hands, and he gives it to the first peasant girl who comes along!* She pulled the diamond ring off her finger and threw it across the room.

There! That's what I think of his presents!

When she looked out the window again, she saw Reggie running toward the girl.

Too late, she thought. A nice gesture, but futile. From where she was standing, it looked like the fireball engulfed them both, plus the girl's father and a couple of reporters standing nearby. The glass in the cabin window shattered and sprayed her with shards, cutting her face and arms in a dozen places. None of the cuts was serious, but blood began to run down her cheeks and arms in long streaks. She couldn't stand to have blood on herself, had gone to great lengths in the past to avoid it, making sure her knife work didn't soil her. She had even paid a doctor to remove her uterus, freeing her of the monthly horror. She hurried over to the sink and splashed water on the cuts, then wiped away the blood with a towel.

It had taken a little bit of precious time, but she was clean and pure again. No reason to let a little mishap spoil the triumph. The situation could still be salvaged. She draped the towel over her shoulder and went out, heading for Reggie's cabin. It was a little further from the explosion and the window was intact. She wrapped the towel around her hand and arm and thrust her fist through the window. She hurriedly knocked out as much of the remaining glass as she could and then climbed inside. There was a worn duffel bag at the foot of the bed. She dumped it out and pawed through the contents. Her heart leaped when she saw the wooden box that contained her knife. She opened the box, withdrew the knife and kissed the blade. She used it to cut a strip of fabric from the bed coverings. She tied the knife to her left forearm, using her right hand and her teeth to pull the knot tight.

Hurry!

Rose spotted the weapons box in the corner of the room. Locked. She knew she could get the box open, but not now—there was no time. As she rushed toward the door, she collided with the bed, banging her knee painfully on the frame. She hit the floor awkwardly, deserted by her dancer's grace. From her vantage point on the floor, she spotted something dark under the bed. She groped for it and came up with a gun, a real one, not a trangun. Trust Reggie to keep a little something handy for emergencies.

Thank you, Reggie. You have not died in vain!

The gun settled into her hand. It was designed for a larger hand than her own. Nevertheless, its balance made it easy to wield as she wrapped her delicate fingers around it. The weight had a cold finality to it, like the stillness of the expression on her face. Even if she couldn't get Gunner with the weapon, maybe she could disable him, and then she could use her knife—even better. She patted the blade tied to her arm.

Rose opened the door of the cabin and slipped out. She stayed near the door and looked around.

How much time has gone by? Am I too late?

The scene was one of confusion. A few people were standing, more were on the ground. She moved between the cabins until she could see the place where Gunner had last been, near the speaking platform. The podium had toppled over and part of it was in splinters. As she watched, the podium shifted and was pushed away by a struggling figure beneath it. It was Gunner. She raised the gun in front of her body with both hands, pointing it at his chest, and squeezed the trigger.

As she did so, another figure, a woman, rose from the ground nearby and knocked Gunner aside. Frustrated, Rose couldn't tell whether she had hit Gunner or not. If she had hit him, it might have been only a grazing shot. She raised her weapon again, but the two had retreated behind the smashed podium. She didn't have a clear line of sight.

A piece of debris rolled noisily across the metal roof of the cabin and fell near Rose. Startled, she took a step backward. A small dart thunked into the ground at her feet, feathers quivering from the impact. If she had not stepped back away from the falling debris, the dart would have embedded itself in her back.

She whirled and saw a man above her on the roof. He was preparing another dart to fire at her. Immediately she retreated into the shack and slammed the door. Her mind put a name to the man, even though he wasn't in costume— it was unmistakably Playful Cat. One of her own family was trying to kill her? Everything was spinning away from her. It was her childhood all over again—she was on her own, no one cared, no one would save her.

For a moment she panicked, thinking she had boxed herself in and there was nowhere to run. She heard scratching noises as the man moved around on the metal roof. Then inspiration hit.

She waited until she heard the next noise, located it, stood underneath, and fired upward with the gun. The bullet cut through the metal. There was a scream followed by a satisfying thud as the man rolled off the roof. When there was no further sound, she opened the door, and cautiously went out.

A powerful hand descended on her shoulder and spun her about. The gun was knocked from her grip and flew several meters away. She lashed out with her foot, aiming at the man's groin. He stepped away in time, but broke his grip on her shoulder to do so. Something was not quite right about the way he moved. As he came toward her again, she saw that he held his left arm tightly across his abdomen. Blood gushed around his fingers. Her shot through the metal roof had served its purpose, even if it hadn't finished him altogether. He stumbled and she danced out of his reach, drawing the knife from its improvised sheath on her left forearm.

It was over quickly, too quickly for Rose, but she had other work to do.

Rose looked about for her target. Gunner was moving, making for the copter. She dived for the gun, rolled, and came up on her feet, firing, once, twice. The bullets missed Gunner and struck the side of the vehicle just as he pulled himself in. The copter sprang into the air.

Cursing, Rose ran back into Reggie's cabin. She used the gun to shoot out the locking mechanism on the weapons box. Inside she didn't find the cache she expected. There was only a coil of rope, a heat-sensitive visor, and some ammunition. It wasn't much, but it would have to do. Back outside, she noted that enough time had passed that organized teams were beginning to work with the blast survivors. Hopefully, no one would notice her as she headed for one of the rented helicopters. She picked the nearest and slipped inside. She was not proficient with the controls but could get by.

Gunner's helicopter was nowhere in sight. There was an ocean of green below. She figured that Gunner would head back toward the river town of Manaus, so she set a course that followed the Rio Negro downstream and flipped on the autopilot.

If the emergency tracer system on her control panel hadn't picked up the beacon from the downed copter, Rose would never have seen the wreck. As it was, she could just barely pick out the thin plume of smoke. There was no clearing to land her own helicopter, but a little thing like that was not going to stop Rose. She set the controls to hover over the river, as close to shore as she dared go without snagging the blades in tree limbs. She wrapped the rope around her waist, tucked in the gun and visor, and stepped out the door. She dropped eight meters feet first into the river.

She came up sputtering and swam for shore as fast as possible. She didn't want to become dinner for whatever creatures hunted these jungle rivers. As she pulled herself out of the water, she heard a cracking noise and turned to look. The helicopter had drifted and caught a limb. It tipped crazily, and the blades dipped into the water. It was dragged down and carried away around a bend in the river. The force of the explosion rippled back through the water to her.

There was no way to return. She could only go forward.

Gunner's copter had not crashed conveniently next to the river. Instead, it was perhaps a kilometer away, but that distance was measured in a straight line above the treetops. Down here, on the forest floor, that kilometer would seem like five.

She slipped the heat-sensitive visor on her head. It would not be much help until she was closer to her target. About half a dozen centimeters in front of her, a holographic projection floated. She ignored the extraneous information it offered and focused on simple compass directions. She formed a mental picture of the things she had seen from the air: the river, the plume of smoke. When she was satisfied that she was facing in the right direction, she took note of the compass and started making her way through the undergrowth of bushes and ferns.

Chapter Thirty-seven

"I owe you my life," Gunner said. It was the first thing he had said to Casey since they had taken off. He had tried, unsuccessfully, to get the controls fully functional. Rose's parting shots had done substantial damage. They were paralleling the river, barely skimming over the occasional trees that projected above the forest canopy like volcanic islands rising out of the ocean.

While he worked, Casey had first wrapped her own leg wound with strips of her ragged pants leg, then bound his nearly-useless left arm tightly against his side, bent at the elbow. The gash in her leg, caused by a sharp edge of some flying piece of debris, had bled in a frightening way, then responded to pressure. It wasn't serious, but it could use stitches. It still oozed gently into the wrap.

Gunner's wound was a through-and-through shot. There was no profuse bleeding. Gunner had grimaced when she handled his arm but uttered no cry or complaint. As the minutes wore on in silence, she began to worry that he was in shock or had a head injury that was not apparent. When he spoke, she shifted in her seat to face him.

"You're the one who got us off the ground, away from that maniac," she responded.

"But you didn't have to get involved. Thank you."

"I know an exclusive story when I see one," she replied. Her attempt at lightness fell flat.

Another few minutes passed in silence. Casey began to think about what he was going through, what had just happened to him. The woman he was supposed to marry had tried to kill him with a bomb and then by shooting at him. He had lost his bodyguard—a good friend, perhaps?—and innocent people had been killed or hurt badly. The little girl and her father, certainly. Gunner had given that child the flower that contained the bomb. He probably blamed himself for that.

He probably blamed himself for not knowing about Rose.

Casey felt her feelings for Gunner deepen moment by moment. The thought flitted through her mind that she liked the person she was becoming. She liked the Casey who loved Gunner.

She leaned across the space between them and kissed him on the cheek.

"What was that for?" he asked.

"Just for being you," she said.

"What do you know about who I am? Practically everything you know about me is a lie."

"So tell me now, tell me the truth. I won't spill the beans. I don't even have my recorder," she said. "Who is Robert Gunner?"

"A man with a dream."

From anyone else, it would have sounded pretentious. She was silent, waiting for him to continue, but the shock of what had just happened turned his thoughts inward. She reached out and placed her hand over his. "I'm here when you want to talk."

He turned to face her, and their eyes met. Underneath his stress, under his pain, physical and emotional, there was a recognition that she wasn't just extending her hand but also her heart. It wasn't much, but she was willing to wait.

An alarm sounded, a strident clanging that jolted Casey

back to the present situation. "What's wrong?" she asked tensely.

Gunner was working the controls, flipping switches rapidly, trying for backup systems, but to no avail.

"Damn!" he exploded. "The altitude stabilizer is out." He punctuated his statement by pounding ineffectually on the control panel with his fist.

"We're going down!"

Chapter Thirty-eight

Wind-in-the-Branches smelled fire. He changed his path, even though it would delay his reunion with Sunshine-Above-Trees, and followed his nose to the source. All who lived in the world would do so, to help, or simply to acknowledge the power of the God of Walking Flames, if that should be the way of things. He crouched, looking at the Bad Thing, that which didn't belong. Small flames licked its sides and thin gray smoke rose into the sky.

Wind-in-the-Branches sensed something contained in it, some power like the fierce white bolts from the sky that sometimes split a tree with a terrible crack. It was a power that raised the hairs on his arms and threatened those within.

He smelled blood and fear, and understood that inside the Bad Thing there were people like himself, who bled and knew fear.

To bring them to a safe place he would have to approach the Bad Thing. Touch it. Smell it and take it inside him.

He thought of turning away and going home to Sunshine-Above-Trees. But then he would not be at peace with himself.

He decided, and ran out to the Bad Thing. He found the bodies immediately. He hoisted the woman onto his back and ran to his hiding place, her weight not slowing him down. He left her in the bushes while he went back for the other. He had to half-carry, half-drag the man's limp body. He heard a noise like thunder. When he turned back to look, it appeared as if the Bad Thing had fallen in on itself, perhaps out of shame at its own existence. It was burning more brightly, but his experienced eye told him that the fire would not spread. The threat was gone.

Gently he examined the bodies. Both were alive, in the kind of deep sleep that happened after a fall from the heights of a tree. They would awaken soon. His hands flew lightly over the wounds, removing the crude wrappings. He tasted a drop of their blood, leaned close and sniffed in the odor of their bodies, analyzing. Then he opened his pack and took out the medicine pouch. Selecting a leaf-wrapped powder by its smell, he poured a small amount into his palm. He spat on it and rubbed his hands together to make a thick paste, which he spread sparingly on the man's wound. He unrolled a different bundle and carefully peeled a large, flat, dried leaf from the top of a stack. This he pressed on the man's arm, kneading it into the paste.

He turned his back on the man and knelt over the woman. Her wound was different, wide open enough to let bad spirits in. He sewed the edges together with a practiced hand, using a delicate needle made from a tree thorn and thread made from fine, teased-apart, strands of vine. He repeated the application of paste. As he was peeling the dried leaf from the stack, he heard a change in the man's breathing and felt the man's gaze on his back. He patted the leaf into place on the woman's leg, stood and turned. The man had propped himself up on his good arm and was watching with interest, but no fear.

Wind-in-the-Branches returned his supplies to the bag. As he was tying it closed, he had a strange thought: the man could not call the creatures of the forest to provide sustenance for himself and his woman. How he knew this, he did not know. But he removed a small skin of water from his pack and placed it on the ground, along with the leaf-wrapped fish he had caught this morning.

He nodded at the man in mute farewell and walked away. He was at peace. He had done all he could, and now it was time to go home.

As he wove his way through the trees, he sang aloud, and let his hunger for Sunshine-Above-Trees grow.

Chapter Thirty-nine

When Gunner regained consciousness, he found himself lying on something yielding and fragrant. For a moment he savored the feeling, then opened his eyes to soft light. The pain in his shoulder was much better. He reached up and felt the area. His fingers connected with something he couldn't recognize, some kind of wrinkled dressing. He sat up, wincing at a pulled muscle in his lower back and an assortment of aches throughout his body that were making themselves known. He saw the copter about twenty meters away. It was upright, but the roof and windshield had collapsed, and it was on fire, sending a thin column of smoke up through the leaves. It was a sullen burn, so evidently the fuel lines and tank were intact. But he could tell at a glance that it wouldn't be doing any more travel, under its own power at least.

He had no memory of how he had gotten out of the copter and over to the bushes. Then his thoughts cleared and he remembered that he hadn't been alone in the copter.

Casey! Did she get out too? He looked around frantically.

She was lying on the ground nearby, still unconscious. Kneeling over her was a small man, brown as a chestnut and nearly naked, running his hands over her leg. Gunner's mind seemed to focus on details of the scene rather than grasping the whole. The vertebrae in the man's back, the fringe of black hair slicked down on his head, the strength and grace of his movements. The tension in the man's shoulders altered. He knew he was being watched.

The man continued to work, drawing what appeared to be a needle through Casey's skin, making swift knots, and biting the thread with his teeth. Then he smeared something on Casey's leg and kneaded some leaves into it. He sat back on his ankles and surveyed his work with evident satisfaction. Only then did he stand and turn toward Gunner.

Their eyes met, and in the filtered light of the forest floor Gunner saw a being who walked in the footsteps of Mother Nature herself, who was lulled to sleep by the steady heartbeat of the earth and awakened by the soft singing of the trees. Gunner felt no fear, only wonder. It was a sight he would remember the rest of his life.

The man gathered up his belongings. A puzzled look crossed his face, and he removed two items from his bag and placed them on the ground. Then, with a nod, he was gone, vanished into the trees.

Gunner stood up, feeling dizzy as he did so. The two items turned out to be a container—made of skin?—of water, and raw fish wrapped up in leaves. As Gunner pondered this evidence of good will, it occurred to him that the man had probably, almost certainly, pulled them from the burning wreckage.

It was the second time Gunner's life had been saved within the hour.

A groan from Casey was a reminder of the here and now. He helped her sit up, her back against a tree trunk, and offered her a sip of water from the skin. He noticed that the pain in his shoulder was decreasing by the minute. His arm was at least usable. When the copter crashed, the emergency beacon must have been activated. Even if it was no longer signaling, a rescue team—his own or the government's—would have gotten a fix on it. Help was on the way and all they had to do was hold out until it arrived. That didn't sound too bad.

If the water in the skin was used up, he could search for a stream or collect rainwater with cupped leaves. The fish was raw, of course. That wasn't at the top of his preference list, but he would eat it, and see that Casey ate it, too, for strength.

Casey. He could not sort out his feelings for the woman, but he promised himself he would, when they got out of this fix. First things first, and that meant getting them out of the forest.

Casey was looking around alertly, rubbing her neck. She caught sight of the paste and leaves on her leg, and looked up, puzzled.

"What . . ."

Gunner leaned against the tree trunk next to her, slipping his good arm around her shoulders. She nestled next to him, putting her head on his shoulder and resting her hand on his thigh as if she had done so a thousand times before.

"Mmm, that's nice," she said. "Now how about telling me what's going on?"

"It seems we have a guardian angel," he began. "We were both knocked unconscious in the crash. When I woke up, there was a native tending to our wounds. I suppose he was one of the Guehero, who live in this area. He must have dragged us away from the copter before the roof fell in and burned. He left food and water, too. He was . . ." For a moment Gunner lost his voice, remembering the man's deep contentment. "I won't forget him."

"I wish I had seen him. I would have liked to thank him. My leg feels terrific, relatively speaking."

"It might sound trite, but he seemed like all of nature in one package."

"Nature. Now why does that remind me of something?" She struggled to get to her feet. He helped her up and saw that she limped, regardless of what she had said about how good her leg felt. "I think I'll go powder my nose."

"Don't go far. It's a jungle out there."

She rolled her eyes and headed away. After a few minutes, Gunner began to worry about her. He was about to set off in the direction she had gone when he heard a rustling noise behind him. He spun about and froze.

"Hello, Robert," Rose said. In one hand she held a gun aimed at his chest, in the other a coil of rope. "Where's your new lady friend?"

"Dead. Burned in the crash." He nodded in the direction of the copter. "I got out just in time." He hoped desperately that Casey could get away, that Rose would believe the story and not go after her.

Rose shrugged, a cold response that chilled him as much as her words. "Spares me the trouble of killing her." Her eyes narrowed. "What's that on your shoulder?"

He realized she meant the paste and leaves. "Something I learned from Reggie," he said. "First aid in the wild, that sort of thing." He tried to keep his voice level. She was wary, standing far enough away to prevent a rushing attack. "Rose, why are you doing this?"

"A family tradition." She laughed, a wild burst that ended abruptly. She gestured with the pistol. "Over there." He moved under a tree with a heavy overhanging branch. "Hold out your hands."

Gunner stood still, defiant. A bullet licked the side of his head at eye level. He twisted away, but not soon enough. A searing pain radiated from the track of the bullet, blurring his vision.

"I said do it!" she shouted.

He held his arms out, hands together. She pressed the gun under his chin with one hand as she deftly looped the rope around his wrists with the other. He found it difficult to think, to plan, with the gun tucked under his jaw. He kept picturing the bullet exiting from his head, like a cartoon character holding a flashlight to one ear and having light shine from the other. Then Rose tossed the end of the rope up over the branch, drawing his hands above his head, and tied the rope securely to the tree trunk. She tucked the weapon into her waistband and hunted around in the underbrush. She came back with a sturdy length of branch, which she held next to the rope. She twisted the rope around one end of the branch and then rotated the branch, like fastening a tourniquet. As she wrapped the rope onto the branch, Gunner was lifted into the air. She stopped when his feet dangled helplessly, bracing the end of the branch in a fork of the tree.

She drew a knife from the cloth band that secured it to her forearm. Gunner saw her approach, but his vision was blackening at the edges from the grazing wound on his head. When she was close enough, he drew up his legs and kicked out at her. She danced away easily.

He would tire soon. He closed his eyes, shutting out the pain as the knife flicked and bit.

I am going to die, and break a lot of promises.

Casey hadn't walked far into the forest when she came across a small stream, a trickle really. She was tempted to go back immediately to show off her find, but decided to accomplish what she came for first. Then she couldn't resist splashing some of the water on her face and arms. It refreshed her, and she began to feel hopeful about an early rescue.

She was almost back to the crash site. She raised her arm to push aside the last bush, and paused. She heard voices. Peering cautiously through the leaves, she caught her breath at the sight of Rose aiming a weapon at Gunner. Casey gasped as Rose fired, grazing the side of Gunner's head. Frantically she tried to think of what to do.

Reggie's gun! Where?

She looked at the smoldering hulk of the copter. It had to be there. She wouldn't even let the thought into her head that it wasn't. She made her way through the bushes to the wreck, hoping that Rose wouldn't opt for a quick kill. Keeping out of sight, she poked into the ruined cabin. She spotted the gun on the floor underneath what was left of the pilot's seat. She picked it up, wincing because the metal was hot from the recent fire. She hoped it was still in working order.

She recognized it as a trangun, like the one she had carried years ago on assignments in unsavory neighborhoods. It was considerably heavier than she remembered a trangun to be, but it had been a long time since she'd used one.

Keeping herself concealed, Casey worked her way close enough to Rose that she didn't think she could possibly miss. She saw Gunner hanging by his wrists, trying repeatedly to connect with his feet, as Rose twirled away almost gaily. Already blood ran from a dozen shallow cuts on his arms and chest. She bit her lip as she waited for Rose to get in the position she wanted, with her back to Casey and far enough away from Gunner. *There!* She squeezed the trigger. There was a loud crack, and the recoil jolted her arms.

Now that was something the tranguns she was familiar with never did.

This one spat out a Baby Blue bullet, whose purpose in life was to bully its way through steel plates and explode on the other side. A small spot of red blossomed below Rose's shoulder blades, spoiling her white blouse. The impact lifted her off her feet and threw her forward. The bullet detonated, churning her insides like butter. A hole opened in her chest, swallowing the skin painting of a perfect rose in early bloom, the bud still tight in the center.

Chapter Forty

Gunner hated hospitals. The only good thing about this one was that he was a visitor, not a patient.

"Dammit, Gunner, slow down. I'm coming as fast as I can!"

He stopped and turned, realizing that he had been pre-occupied and was walking too fast. Casey came stumping up, walking with a cane. In the three days since the wild flight into the forest, her leg had recovered very well, thanks to a man with a thorn for a needle and a bundle of dried leaves. His own shoulder was healing astoundingly well. Already, new pink skin was stretched over the wound. The medical personnel in the rescue team had chattered excitedly over the paste and leaves, almost forgetting their patients.

Before nightfall the rescue team had showed up, dropping down from two hovering helicopters. The rescuers had found the two of them huddled together near the wreckage, as far away from Rose's body as they could get. Even in the few short hours that her corpse lay on the ground, ants and other scavengers had started their work, marring the beautiful woman who was once his bride-to-be.

He pushed open the door to Room 342, holding it open for Casey. Inside, in a drug-induced sleep, was Reggie.

He had lost one arm to the shoulder, one leg to the knee, and half of his face. What wasn't broken was charred. That he survived at all was due to a protective bodysuit he had put on that morning, in spite of the heat, complaining to

Gunner that his balls were stewing in sweat. Premonition? Or simply the discipline of the trade? It didn't matter which. The bodysuit had absorbed some of the shock of the blast, spreading it out in its layers of gel and air.

It was an advantage the little black-haired girl and her father didn't have. He'd promised the girl's mother that he would open a free clinic on the spot they'd died, to care for all the families in the area. It wasn't much, but it was the best he could do.

Reggie would be in the hospital for weeks, maybe months. His burns and internal injuries would heal, prosthetic limbs would be fitted, the finest available, ones that would respond to his own nerve impulses. Cosmetic surgery would reshape his face.

It was a miraculous process, akin in Gunner's mind to bringing back the dead.

Casey slipped her hand into his, reminding him that some promises were more pleasant to keep than others.

Chapter Forty-one

The man in the clown costume stood. The discussion was over. The spotlight shone down on him harshly, providing no concealing, forgiving shadows. Around the granite conference table there were three others, seated in cones of light; two chairs were empty. He held each of their gazes briefly. Cold-Blooded Serpent, Chess Master, Wrongful Death.

"I formally propose," Tearful Clown said, "that The Six be disbanded and that each member remain silent about our past activities."

Chess Master leaned forward, placing his elbows on the table. The light glinted from his crown.

"You mean break up and shut up," he said.

"You always did have a way with words," Tearful Clown said. "You have to admit we nearly made a serious mistake with Gunner."

"But will this Coalition for the Earth be effective?" Chess Master pressed. "Effectiveness is important."

Tearful Clown gave the question serious consideration, for himself as well as for the earnest figure in the crown and purple robe.

"Yes," he said. "Yes, I believe it will be." The diamond in the center of the tear painted on his cheek flashed as he nodded his head. "Vote."

There was a small chorus of ayes.

"The proposal is carried." Tearful Clown honked his red bulb nose. He wondered if the costumed people at the table would follow the resolution, or carry on their murderous work individually and secretly.

Were they capable of stopping?

Was he?

"Good-bye, all," he said, as he let the darkness at the edge of the room draw him away.

Adam Grant sat in his chair on the porch of his country home, watching the crocuses sway in the early spring breeze, brave yellow spots of cheer in a landscape still sleepy-eyed with winter. The breeze brought exciting news, the tantalizing fresh scent of blossoms and bees already stirring further south, the promise of renewal, as it did every spring. But this year was different. This year, renewal had taken on a new meaning.

The breeze gently dried the tear that had been poised on his cheek for the past thirty years. Sarah came out with a tray. There was a deep satisfaction in her face he hadn't seen for years.

"Have some tea, dear," she said. "It'll warm your heart and put some life in those old bones."

And it did.